93 Degrees

To: Steve

Ken Rugland

To: Steve

93 Degrees

By Ken England

ISBN 978-0-615-71108-9

This novel is dedicated to my parents Ruth and Bob England, they taught me how to love. And they are the truly grounding influence in my life.

CHAPTER 1

Yucca bristled needle-sharp and defensive like star bursts in the sun. A cottontail exploded in a blur of brown, flipped a corner and leaped into a zig. A safety route zagged the animal back from the approaching human.

Southwestern high desert unfolds for miles. The runner maintains a determined pace on a steep switch back climb. As the angle of the land levels the runner takes a pause to breath and enjoy the view. The trail now level, dropped into the approach of a slot canyon, which paralleled the path and intersected Bruja Canyon.

The side slot had shaped a unique gap not found in most canyon rock. Instead of abrupt edges and vertical walls; this opening eases down into a forty-five degree angle
The rock on top of the slope is white from mineral deposits left by eons of water; the flowing liquid has eroded the less enduring red sandstone beneath. After the forty five degree slope the canyon plummets vertically to the canyon floor thirty feet below and at the bottom is a plunge pool, which is black and still, as if waiting.

The temptation to briefly stop and take in the the unusual sight teased the female runner's mind once more but engorged muscle took charge and raced on into freedom. Tense shoulder and back muscles loosened with each stride. The rhythm of the run spreads joy to every moving cell and on; into the very essence of her soul. Sharply focused eyes calculate twists and turns as the trail edged closer to the chasm's rim.

The descent dropped steeper until effortless strides shorten and the pace becomes measured. Half way to the end of the canyon, she's takes notice of the dry creek bed in the small slot canyon that intersects with Bruja Canyon. At this precise moment she encounters a fish hook cactus guarding a four foot drop into an eroded gully.

The twenty-three year old veers her body weight slightly to avoid the spines of the cactus and instead of landing solidly on the ground, the outer edge of her right running shoe glances on the loose gravel. Her torso, still in motion commenced a fall as her ankle gives way. It's as if a carpet has been jerked out from under her.

The clarity of the incident immediately blurs. Was it her mental fatigue from the night before, the loose gravel on the hard pack, or that lurking fish hook cactus that laid her low; the
why's crash through her mind. The fall is recorded in her subconscious mind as her head feels a sharp blow.

As she rolls down the forty-five degree slope, her body takes a beating, her hip screams out in pain, followed by the base of her skull; snapped back from the impact. Instantaneously the body twists into a frantic slide head first. The acceleration down the rocky slope allows her little time to contemplate the black hole fast approaching.

The bicolored rock gap is well-eroded and gleams smooth like polished china. In spite of self defense posturing that dictates stretched arms and straightened legs in a desperate attempt to create enough friction for a stop or slowing; Chiara continues the slide and is forced to look directly into certain painful death.

His eyes rolled in REM sleep. The dream was short but disturbing. Chiara was in a concrete jail cell. Or was she? In the dream, the wall colors seemed too vibrant for a concrete room.

The sound of the woman calling for help pulled at him. Why was she in a jail cell? The question turned over in his mind.

His twenty-four year old body sprawled muscular; tanned and tangled in the sheets. A tattoo of black thorns circled the carved left bicep. Nothing moved in the room except the rhythmic rise and fall of his back with each breath. Soft morning sun peeked into the window and dust particles drifted lazily through the first tiny shaft of light. Steg, the black cat sat on the headboard with half lidded eyes. On occasion they flared open like yellow-green flames; as if to scan the room for signs of life from his owner or from his dreams.

The adobe wall above the purring cat tethered a dream catcher woven with braided leather. A turquoise stone placed off-center seemed lost in the string leather web. The stone's blueish- green color was the same color of Chiara's eyes and that was the reason Jason had originally noticed and bought it.

Chiara Martinez had not planned to travel to the womb of the earth. The slide direction had delved her off the place where the actual canyon bed intersects the edge of the slippery slope; known as a 'pour off'. It is a place where water pours into the canyon during seasonal cloudbursts.

Unable to emit a full scream; time slows and the drama of it all pushes small guttural whimpers from her mouth.

As her body approached the intersection Chiara was turned ninety degrees into the fall line. She summoned every once of strength to keep from rolling like a log; the rock edge hit's her squarely in her ribs. And with a loud "Uoof" air is expelled forcefully from her lungs.

The fall is halted, but only temporarily. Her legs fail to land on the flat surface near the rock lip, but instead swing free over the edge. That momentum compels the rest of her body to peel off the savior rock under her arm. In spite of her best effort she plunges; free falling. Nothing but atmosphere courses around her body.

A lifetime later the ice cold water smacks her body, mind and soul. She remembers only the furiously cold plunge. Her feet end the fall on the mud-sand bottom of the waterfall pool.

Chiara automatically pushes off to bolt up and out of the water. Her mouth opens in a silent scream followed by a hollow whining as her damaged ribs remember how to function. Three gasps force her panic to disperse. Slow efforts allow enough muscle relaxation around her lungs to encourage small amounts of air; just enough to stay conscious.

"Oh shit!" she hissed.

Jason rarely remembered his dreams but somehow this one stuck. She called his name again as the dream ends.

Straining to see, his eyes startle open pulling him from the REM sleep; then clench shut.

Cautiously he crossed the zone between sleep and wakeful; his stomach lurched at the bright light. He felt the dream sensation imprint on his body.

He moved to his back and turned his head to find Chiara. But the space beside him held no warm graceful female. This was of little concern; his girlfriend hadn't been sleeping well in the past month's and often left the bed before he awakened. Just last night, she was pensive bordering on despondent due to an event at the hospital.

Chiara Martinez and Jason Bactiere had met as river guides three years before, on the Grand Canyon. It was a year after the Gulf war.

The two year stint in the military had just ended and Jason, newly discharged, waited in Saudi Arabia for well earned civilian freedom as the conflict dissolved. After discharge he swore never to live in a desert again, but within six months, at the urging of a friend, he found himself rafting the Grand Canyon. That Colorado River trip led him to Chiara. Their time as river guides began a significant relationship between them; one that balanced the harshness of the previous desert experience.

Jason admired Chiara's unique combination of strength and beauty. She ran trails in the high desert like a wild thing. She was true and complete in the dry and dramatic natural environment. She could travel great distances on rugged trails without obvious effort. During the shared runs he became motivated and stimulated by the pursuit of that fast woman. He ran hard and continued with futile attempts to keep up with her fleeting form.

Often he accelerated around a bend in full run, determined to find her right around the next rock just beyond his reach; only to find her relaxing into a sexy leg stretch with a carefree smile as if waiting for him. Or was it just to tease him, he wondered? She understood the primal chase modality from the predator and prey angle.

When he did catch up with her, she would fall into his powerful arms. And he knew she wanted to be there because he only caught her when she wanted to be caught. And that often lead to an extended time of foreplay which culminated in lovemaking, often right there in the desert environment.

The desert appeared to embrace and support her every whim. No trails were steep enough or rough enough to slow her gazelle like stride. Sharing time with her in those rarely touched by human landscapes, shifted his deep war memories into a place of clean desert sun and crystal.

But lately mysterious clouds curled into their daily horizons.

The preceding evening when she arrived home from her shift at the emergency room in the Mesquite Hospital; a muted auburn haired young woman moved into his open arms for the customary welcome home greeting.

He leaned down to look into her blue eyes just before the kiss, but immediately tears shimmered into the blue eyes like the turquoise in the dream catcher. He could see and feel that she needed him to hold her now without delay.

The afternoon meeting with a young patient had left a gloomy mark on her soul.

The moment his arms circled her, a great sigh escaped. He held tighter. Mere seconds passed before the wide, yet feminine shoulders shook with unspent sobs. Minutes later, her immediate grief spent, he teased the story out of her with gentle encouragement.

"What happened at work tonight?" His voice was quiet and respectful.

"I just realized I probably wasted the last four years of my life in nursing school." she choked out, wiping her eyes on her sleeve.

"I happen to know that's not true, you are a great nurse and one of the most compassionate people I know!" Jason said.

"That's the problem."

"Go on." he urged with as much concern as he could muster on short notice and only part of the story.

"There was a three year old towheaded boy with the most beautiful eyes. He's been diagnosed with a rare form of cancer," Tears welled again as the memories swarmed her.

"I had to start the I.V. line before he was even admitted into the hospital for surgical removal of a tumor.....but . . ." another sob cut her off.

Jason reached out to help her through the silence. "Well you helped him then."

"When I inserted the needle, his eyes spilled tears even though he tried so hard to hold them back." she sighed deeply, "and this is just the beginning of his lost innocence," she said, quietly shaking her head, those sweet young eyes will never see the world the same again," She pulled his arms from her shoulders.

"Where is the justice in this world, Jason?" She moved toward the bathroom. "I need a shower."

Later, Chiara drank a cup of tea as she pulled together the coffee for the next morning, as an RN coffee was never far from her mind. She set the automatic timer on the coffee pot and then went directly to bed without saying anything more about her day. Jason hoped the tea and hot shower would soothe her wounded heart and the next morning would improve her emotions. She had made plans for a big run tomorrow because she had the day off.

But that night he felt Chi toss and turn numerous times in bed; struggling again with her demons. She had a giving heart that struggled to keep the work separated from her emotions during her RN work. Eventually he fell into a fitful sleep beside her.

The following morning he lay in bed warming in the sun light and his mind drifted back over the last few months. He recalled more than a few episodes of cavernous sadness that seemed to appear out of nowhere every few weeks. In between the episodes she would rebound and become the sweet, happy-go-lucky girl full of life and fun that he remembered from summers on the Colorado River. She had worked summers to pay for nursing school at UNLV. She had graduated three months before and started right way working for the Emergency Department in Mesquite, Nevada.

Before his military service, Jason Bactiere had been an up and coming competitive climber. It was an activity that rarely paid the bills so he worked the Grand Canyon during the tourist season. He was presently unemployed and spent many of his days climbing the nearby crags. He dabbled with the possibility of authoring a guide book for the local climbing areas; however the days when Jason wasn't climbing he was looking for work at one of the casino's in Mesquite. At first Jason was disappointed that he wasn't earning any money and was relying on Chiara. But once they had a long talk and decided they were a team in this life, he felt much better.

The red LED alarm clock read ten A.M. when he finally half rolled, half hopped out of bed.

"Find work soon," he muttered to himself.

A lithe Spartan body honed from ten years of climbing at the edge of his ability, flexed and he stood. Muscles ached with lactic acid built up from working several hours on yesterday's climb. However the secrets of this climb continued to elude him even after months of similar attempts. He lived to unlock the rock's secrets currently on that climb.

But now the pressing issue was to empty his bladder. His stomach vied for attention and breakfast needed to happen soon. He left the bathroom to walk across a cold concrete floor then did a quick survey of the small two bedroom adobe structure. He walked back to the bedroom, slipped on a shirt and some pants, then moved out to the living room, but no Chiara. He walked back through the living room, swung the front door open and felt the grip of dread. Chiara's yellow Subaru was gone.

CHAPTER 2

The child's eyes were glossy and his small jaw bone locked into place to keep it from quivering. Then there was another face; an elderly man with a neatly trimmed beard saying something to the child.

Chiara couldn't see. It was as if there was a hat over her eyes that she had to keep pushing up.

The man was speaking to the child and Chiara leaned forward to better hear.

"Do not fear," the older man said, "Dying is the easy part . It's like a long sleep; living is the hard part."

Chiara watched as the child took the elder's hand to walk away into a bright white fog.
She wanted to reach out and take the child's hand and say no but she couldn't move or speak.

Steg sat on her chest; his purr slow and low. Those night vision eyes stared intently at her fluttering lashes. She shifted him down to the floor and then lay back for a moment, to
think about the dream.

A shiver passed through her at the memory of the cold white fog. Sitting up, her feet dropped to search the floor. She found the flip-flops and stood quietly to look back at Jason, who hadn't moved.

She had been doing this off and on all night; tossing and turning, looking at the clock. The glance now told her it was finally time to get up. Five-thirty in the morning; no point to stay in bed at this hour , she thought.

Chiara walked out to the kitchen and sat at the table to think. In the past she found the best stress reliever was exercise. There was no work tomorrow, but the sporadic events with the child had left her tired. After yesterday's work she really needed a ten mile run and since she had tomorrow to recover she decided to go. She quickly gathered the necessities for a long run.

Steg jumped up onto the table to stare silently, watching her every move.

"I wish I could be more like you sometimes," she spoke to the cat as she jotted a note for Jason, "Life is a lot less complicated for you isn't it? Lucky cat. You behave now, and don't wake Jason."

The dependable old engine started and Chiara drove across the gravel lot to access the highway. The town of Littlefield passed by promptly in the meager light. She thought she saw someone on the porch of a house, slowly swaying back and forth in a rocking chair. It struck her as odd that someone might be lounging on the porch at this early hour.

Within thirty minutes she arrived at the parking area of the Virgin River Gorge climbing area, known to the climbers as The Gorge.

By the time she parked the car a pinkish-glow of dawn streaked wispy clouds that hung up in the morning sky. A number of climbers who lived in the area a good part of the year were gathered around a campfire. She made a point to stay as far from the climbers as possible.

Chiara sat in her car with eyes closed wishing for anonymity today. Any kind of people would get in the way of this run, and especially people that she knew. She needed the challenge and solitude of nature to set her mind and heart straight.

Jason knew most of these climbers before he and Chiara had connected. She'd been around them enough to know this morning she wasn't up for their banter. She searched for other options.

Bruja Canyon was a favorite of hers. Even though the name was Spanish for witch; she was fascinated with the high sandstone walls and drawn-out chasms.

She and Jason had climbed there before. She knew all the trails but there was one trail she had yet to run. The early start made today a good day to check it out . If she left now she could be there just after sunrise and should have plenty of time to explore this unknown Upper Trail.

The climbers around the campfire saw the headlights of the car as it pulled up. Rather than a door opening, the lights came back on and the car pulled out of the parking area to the roadway.

"Isn't that the kind of car Chiara Martinez drives?" the first climber asked.

"You mean Jason's girlfriend?" replied another climber.

"Yeah it might be her."

"I don't know it's kind of dark out here."

Chiara arrived at the mouth of Bruja Canyon at seven fifteen in the morning. The sun lifted over the distant hill tops and eliminated the morning chill. A Bloodroot tree grew by the side of the canyon; in full bloom, it would provide excellent shade for the car as the heat of the day increased.

The actual entrance to the canyon was blocked against vehicle access by a split rail fence with a locked gate. From past climbing trips to this place she knew that the land owners permitted hikers, climbers and non-motorized explorers only.

As she stepped out into the sweet fragrance of the Bloodroot blossoms, the old Subaru engine made it's normal clicking noises while it cooled. The desert is quiet. Nothing moves. The wind hasn't picked up yet but the temperature is already on the rise.

"This run will be a workout," Chiara thought. A switchback trail climbed up a talus slope that poured out of a break in the canyon wall. The path led up to the canyon's south rim then continues west for approximately five miles as it zigzags in and out of mulltiple side canyons only to returbn back on the north side.

Her ritual includes warm up tendon stretches; she continues to scan the canyon wall. She thinks it was a good decision to run this trail today.

Weariness nags her but it wasn't long until the adrenaline began to work it's magic. Her fingers tether the laces taut on the New Balance Trail Runner shoes. She pulls the shoulder length hair back and secures it with a hair tie. As if going over a checklist she systematically inspects the small fanny pack beginning with a ritualistic deep breath.

It contains a quart bottle of water, an energy bar and car keys that are stowed in a pocket. She makes the decision not to carry the nylon windbreaker because she hates running with any thing extra.

A second breath later she slips the windbreaker over her head in a rush that pushes a hair barrette from the jacket pocket into the sand. Tossing the windbreaker into the front seat she locks the door and concentrates on the familiar and automatic oxygen load that floods her capillaries with a third deep breath.

Chiara loved trail running because it centers her mind. As she tops out on the rim of the canyon, running with small steps and sucking in quarts of oxygen with each breath; major endorphins release along with large portions of negative events and emotions from the preceeding day. The little boy fades from her awareness.

The view from the canyon edge opens her. The trail levels off and Chiara settles into a moderate stride amid generations of ancient desert dwellers, now long gone that had perfected this way of safe, economical and swift travel across this landscape.

The panoramic canyon scene beckons her soul. How did it get that name she wondered; the gash in the desert floor known as Bruja Canyon. What is the first story of how it got named? What did a witch have to do with it, anyway?

From this distance, Bruja Canyon appears to run out into a plateau that had lifted in the ancient past; thus allowing eons of sporadic water to sculpt it. Water makes all canyons true natural art forms of the desert; but this particular gorge is spectacular in a unique way.

Bruja had a fresh water spring at the head of the canyon, thus the name Bruja Ojo which the Spanish word for spring. The spring provided a continuous year-round and unfettered flow of water the full length of the canyon. Her plan for the day included a break at the spring to refill her water bottle.

She moved across the plateau surrounded by the desert flora growing out of the red hard-packed ground. Amid various other plants she saw yellow desert grasses, tall spindly Ocotillo cactus bushes and the occasional spiked-out Joshua trees. Each yucca defended it's territory with a nasty force field of spines as many a desert hiker had inadvertently and painfully discovered.

The tanned fit figure of the woman moved without difficulty down the trail. At this segment of the path, not much more than a light colored line appeared in the red dirt, barely wide enough for her foot. Chiara trotted on, mesmerized and comforted by the wide open spaces; big enough to hold the grief she felt for that blameless child.

Mountains ranged out to swaddle her from every perspective; then rose on each horizon only to fade, one by one, into distant nothingness. Each stride into the canyon carried her out of the pain of the young boy that watched a needle impale his arm and his life.

Jason stepped further out the door, coffee in hand to stand on the cement step; keen for a glimpse of the yellow Subaru on the horizon. He and Chiara drank their coffee out here when they could. He scanned the small community surrounding their adobe house.

The elderly schizophrenic woman paced a spot near her self-imposed post by the Littlefield, Arizona welcome sign. She jabbered to passing cars or unseen spirits; all the while gesturing with her arms. She had been a fixture at this triangle where two different state highways blended together for the last ten years. The woman was a slightly overweight, unkept woman who could not make eye contact with anyone. She wore the same baggy dress every day, rain or shine. She somehow succeeded in escaping the eyes of mental health professionals in the three bordering states of Arizona, Nevada, and Utah.

Littlefield was a sleepy town in the high desert of northeastern Arizona. The town is a cultural mix of Caucasians and Hispanics; most of whom are somehow involved in agriculture. And right on the border of the Paiute Wilderness.

Jason had located this rental house in Littlefield, Arizona after the last river rafting season. It was within the couple's price range and because it is a comfortable commuting distance to Chiara's job they signed a lease. They were on a tight budget until they got their feet on the ground financially. The most attractive aspect of the adobe for

Jason was the scattered sandstone cliffs adjacent to the town in this region of the southwest desert country.

Jason sipped the last shot of coffee and gave one more scan of the horizons searching for any sign of a dust trail generated by Chiara's car. There were various dirt roads leaving the town. His eyes found nothing and assumed she had departed just after dawn. Re-entering the house he went to the kitchen for more coffee and saw the note. He hesitated for a moment , trepidation sinking through him,and then leaned over to read it.

Chiara's flowing handwriting graced the page :

"Jason, I went for a run. I just needed to get out and think and try to shake the world off my back. I think I'll go to the Gorge so I'll be at least 4-5 hours. Later, Chi."

He smiled at the way she signed off using his pet name for her, even though when he first called her that she professed a dislike for it. He found a slice of cold pizza in the refrigerator; collected his coffee and headed back outside to survey the morning and think some more. His preferred seat was on the concrete slab which served as a porch, outside the front door of the house; or the stoop as they called it back east.

The house sat on a half acre but in the past, the barren lot had been used without limitation as an access for all number of vehicles. The extremes of the desert environment eradicated any chance for vegetative growth. A twenty yard expanse of small yellow gravel, native to this area, surrounded the house like a ring of pale blonde moonlight.

Steg slipped out the open door purring shamelessly and came over to lean against Jason's side. He sought affection at every opportunity because his owners were outdoor oriented and could rarely be found inside the house for long. Jason picked the cat up with both hands and held him up in front of his face. Black cat body dangled in the fresh morning air.

"Steg, why didn't you wake me up when your mom was leaving?" Jason asked the feline. Steg responded with a stifled meow.

"You know we have to take care of her, cause she's kinda sad," he said.

He settled the cat down into his lap so he could scratch behind his ears and encourage the contented meows. He enjoyed hearing the cat talk. However, not appreciating the sentiment, Steg darted off half way across the gravel lot; then crouched as if stalking an imaginary ground squirrel.

The practice of hunting for a black cat around this house was a challenge considering the light colored gravel and lack of cover for a good long distance in any direction. As he watched the cat fidget and slink, Jason wondered if maybe Steg saw the same invisible spirits as the woman over by the welcome sign. Sometimes she twitched too.

The lazy morning sun climbed higher and hotter as Jason drank more coffee and thought back over the last few months of his time with Chiara.

He wasn't particularly knowledgeable about medical issues, especially those of the mind, and they lived such an active life that subtle problems were especially difficult to detect.

At moments of quiet like this, more than a few occurrences of her sadness bubbled into his mind. She had no interest in any activity, including sex which was ordinarily an enjoyable activity for both of them. She had little to say and even less expression on her face during those gloomy days. In fact there was one entire week when she could barely get up off the couch. He wondered if he had missed some obvious clue or fact, which would help define the mystery of her behavior changes. He was noticing a definite cycling pattern, or was he?

"More of those invisible spirits," he said to the now absent Steg. Standing up from the step to stretch, he felt the soreness in his triceps. He waited back into the house and looked at the note again.

"Maybe I'll make a trip down to the Gorge after all there are a few climbs I've been working on there," He would do his best to fill up a day without Chiara. He hated to admit how much he missed her when she took off on a lone run.

"Who can I roundup to come along?" He said to himself then reached for the phone and punched in a number.

Tommy Perkins rolled over in bed to the third ring of his phone, or was it the fourth?

"Yeah?" he replied curtly with more indignation than greeting or question.

"Tommy. It's Jason. Let's head out to the Gorge and pull down a couple of routes."

"Jesus Christ man! Are you stoned? You damn near killed me yesterday."

"Stop your whinning, what if you die tomorrow? What are you going to tell Saint Peter, that you're a pussy?" Jason said with a grin stretching across his face. He always enjoyed a little verbal wrangling with Tommy.

"Saint Peter? Dude, I think the guy's name at my gate would be Satan."

Jason howled with laughter.

"Seriously man, I can barely lift my arms, I may need a month off," Tommy said.

"Oh, please Everyone knows you could dust half the crowd out there," Jason rebutted.

"That may be, but climbin' don't pay me a dime and if I ain't at work in a hour; the Man ain't going to pay me a dime either," he said with finality in his voice.

"Okay man, but if I send 'Boundaries' today you'll never forgive yourself."

"So, if you don't have a climbing partner are you gonna solo Boundaries?"

"Yeah, I'm pretty solid on it."

"Be careful I don't want to be at a funeral tomorrow, and I don't need another black mark on my record when I walk through the Gates of Hates."

"You know, Tommy, I'm not the sit around and just let life happen, kinda guy."

"Okay, don't do anything stupid, and thanks for being my alarm clock this morning."

"Don't mention it dude have a good day at work."

"Yeah Jason, be safe out there dude."

The phone clicked off and Jason walked into their spare bedroom which doubled as a warehouse for a multitude of outdoors sports. He grabbed a swami belt, a chalk bag, climbing shoes and his walkman, thinking that he may solo a few moderate routes.

Next he looked around for clean clothes and spied a pile of dirty laundry in the corner settling into the angle of repose. He decided quickly that he would have to do laundry today-but only after he found Chi. Then he slipped into a dirty pair of spandex tights and a tank top and shoved the remaining pile into a big duffel bag and grabbed it on the way out.

In the kitchen he filled a water bottle, grabbed a few power bars and made sure a window was open for the Stegosaurus. He dragged the duffel bag out, glanced quickly around as he left the house. He flipped the back window open on his pickup topper and tossed the bag in the back. Within minutes the faded red Toyota pickup with a bent tailgate hummed away from the house.

CHAPTER 3

"Mr. Scapalini?" asked Jack King as he entered the finely detailed office on the tenth floor of the Crown Jewels Casino. Mahogany covered walls and long red satin drapes hung from the fifteen foot ceiling; western facing windows opened to a panorama of desert landscape.

"Now that's a view. One day all that will become a beautiful housing development, if I have my way," said a voice from the leather chair facing the windows.

The chair spun around and a man with dark hair, angular features and small dark eyes faced him.

"Jack how was your adventure into the desert?" asked Joey Scapalini. He exhaled a large puff of cigar smoke and gazed at the broad shouldered, square jawed man who had just entered his office.

Joey had acquired the casino after being excommunicated from his syndicate family in the Atlantic City area. He moved to Las Vegas, five years ago with a truck full of money; partly from his fathers' business, partly from high earnings on a wildly rising stock market. Even a truck load of money was still not enough to break into the hotel and casino business in Las Vegas. His money could buy a piece of real estate in Vegas, but wouldn't pay the wage of an architect to design a casino. Joey had been pretty much laughed out of Vegas. So he stumbled on down the road and landed in second rate Mesquite, Nevada.

It was a small town of fifteen thousand people just inside the Nevada state line. At first, Joey wouldn't even consider the place but after a few business partners spent time cajoling him, telling him he could become the BIG DOG in Mesquite, his fantasy kicked in and he started it all with the purchase of an abandoned grocery store which would become the casino and a hotel would go up behind that.

The next night he dreamed he was Bugsy Segal' with all the media hype and fanfare, arriving in Mesquite, Nevada.

"Give me some good news, Jack," Joey said. He talked while adjusting his collar giving Jack the impression that he was uncomfortable in the monkey suit.

"Nothing but good news, sir," said Jack knowing that good news was rare in this business.

"That's why I hired you Jack, you make my life easy."

From the brown leather chair in front of Joey's desk, Jack leaned forward slightly and then nodded as he spoke.

"I have a friend from my military days; he worked with the Army Corps of Engineers. You give this guy a D9 Cat and he could put Mt. Everest on the back lot of this casino."

"All I need now is some cheap water, Jack."

Joey Scapalini carried a monkey on his back since he opened the casino ten years ago. Westerners in the United States were perpetually held hostage by water availability and with Las Vegas growing at an astronomical rate, water consumption was going through the the roof; as was the cost of the water. Mesquite was situated out in the desert and had to get water pumped in from Vegas, at top dollar prices. The growth of the town was limited by available water. He, who controlled the water, controlled the town.

"It won't be cheap up front, but if you can pull this off, you will be King of this mountain," Jack said, with an air of confidence in his voice.

"So what did your friend think after checking the thing out?"

"The canyon is about ten miles north of here and it has a relatively narrow mouth; if a guy could dam the canyon, by rough calculations it could hold as much as thirty million gallons of water."

"How long would it take to fill that much water?" Joey asked.

"With just normal runoff it would take many years," said Jack. "But get this; the canyon has a year round spring that cranks out enough water to fill the whole damn thing in a couple years."

Knowing that in his world, every silver cloud has a black lining; Joey then asked,

"What are the down sides?"

"The canyon is part of a ranch that is owned by a Mormon fellow named Joseph Rains."

"Well he's got the right name!" Joey said. He grinned broadly and examined his cigar, pleased with himself.

"Yeah, hopefully it makes life easier as a desert rancher," Jack said, playing dumb but knowing full well what Joey had meant.

"Not his last name, his first name!" Joey retorted, gazing over his cigar. He knew Jack was playing mind games, as he usually did. Each man continually tried to out wit the other.

"Oh. Sorry boss," Jack said and casually looked away.

By forty years of age Jack King had spent fifteen years in the Army; the last of those years in the Special Forces. On more than one occasion, he found himself running into trouble with the law. Eventually, he ended up working security at the casino, where Joey Scapalini "discovered" him. It didn't take long for the casino owner to recognize the multiple talents of Jack King and he moved him up from working.as a security guard to the head-of-security position.

While he served with many great commanders in the military, he understood incompetent leaders and disdained them. Jack didn't like Joey Scapalini but he was in a pinch and chose to remain in this pseudo submissive role to avoid a possible prison stay; or worse. And he had to admit, the fringe benefits were attractive; good money, girls, and a little adventure now and then. He figured he had been in many difficult situations in the past and he could tolerate this for a few years.

"Just remember who signs your checks, smart ass," Joey Said.

He stood and walking around the highly polished mahogany desk, stopped just close enough to the head of security's chair to allow odorous morning breath to fall on the back on Jack's neck.

"Have I ever shown you my collection of swords, Jack?" he hissed in a low voice.

"I don't believe so sir," Jack said wondering where this was going.

Joey walked over to the opposing wall and pushed a hidden button. Jack stood to watch two mahogany panels slide back revealing twenty gleaming swords.

"The one on the top left there, Jack, is a Scottish Claymore and you'll recognize this one," he said as he gently removed a blade from the bottom.

"This is from West Point; one of the officers decided he didn't need it any more. If you know what I mean?" He walked back from the sword case to stop near Jack. The West Point blade waved back and forth, inches from Jack's face.

Jack now knew that Joey was compensating for, some insecurity. Time passed slowly. Jack waited quietly, ready to spring if need be, all the while showing no fear.

Joey Scapalini had worked up to a high position that asserted a large amount of control over the garbage industry in Atlanrtic City. His father was the patriarch of the syndicate which illegally ran the business. Joey was the oldest son, therefore would inherit the power position.

There was a painting of the elder Scapalini on the northern wall of the office.

When he was a young man, he had survived an attack which left a bullet lodged in his back. It earned him the name 'The Kevlar Kid'. Later, as the garbage wars were heating up, the senior Scapalini lived up to the name by denying the grim reaper two more times. All told , he had been shot five times and at the time of his death he still carried three slugs inside him.

Joey fell from prominent power when he was tagged a suspect in the disappearance of a few garbage kingdom competitors. No bodies were ever found so Joey was never arrested.

However, his father was later indicted for racketeering and during that trail he died of a massive heart attack due to stress.The garbage kingdom competition saw this opportunity as the perfect time to push Joey, thus the Scapalini mob, out of the city. The steady pressure was more than Joey could take. Fearing for his life, he chose to move out west and eventually set up shop in Mesquite. In Joey's mind the past was never far behind, so even now, ten years later, he was frequently on edge.

Joey gripped the sword handle with both hands. The cigar wedged back in his molars as he locked eyes with Jack to say, "You military guys go around killing people, legally."

He moved the sword slowly, as if testing the weight of a baseball bat.

"How many people have you killed Jack?"

"Hard to say sir."

"Oh come on Jack, don't you guys put notches on your M-16's?"

"Some guys may have."

"You're being modest; I know you're a warrior. That's why we get along so well."

"By necessity,Sir."

Joey laughed and felt secure in the knowledge that he was in complete control of his kingdom.

"Okay," Joey said, "back to business."

Then he walked back around to his desk to lean the West Point sword against it. "I want you to go back to that canyon, find this guy Joseph Rains and feel him out. Find out what it would take to acquire that canyon."

"Yes sir," Jack said, turning to leave .

"What no salute?' Joey said with a booming laugh.

Joey stopped and began to turn back.

"Okay, just a joke, get out of here." Joey said grinning.

Jack left the room stretching his neck, turning his head to stop the grinding of his teeth. Could anyone in the casino hear his teeth masticating his anger as he walked down to the garage?

CHAPTER 4

The Gorge was a state park just on the Arizona side of the state line. It was commonly considered a sport climbing haven and climbers around the country often used it as a winter base of operations. Climbing had seen a cyclic evolution from the early days where climbers used iron spikes called pitons, that were hammered into cracks and the safety rope was attached to prevent life ending falls.

Then the push to environmental responsibility, the rock damaging use of pitons gave way to rock friendly equipment and that trend stuck for twenty years. By the mid eighties European influence swung back to the permanently installed protection known as bolts that were drilled into the rock. This historical technique was widely adopted in most area's over the objections of environmentalists, and was known as sport climbing.

Jason pulled into the parking area of the Gorge, officially known as The Virgin River Gorge, at just after one P.M.

As fall swept across the country like a long slow sunset, the days moved into perfect temperatures for climbing in the high desert. He shut the engine off, got out of the cab and walked over to a man and woman sitting in canvas chairs around the ashes of a burned out campfire.

"Hey Jason," said the man with dusty blonde hair and a soul patch below his bottom lip.

"Kyle, how's it hanging?" asked Jason."

"Like a dog," Kyle replied, to scattered chuckles. In climbing circles a 'hang dog' is a person who continually tries a climb unsuccessfully and ends up hanging on the rope after every attempt.

"Hi Rose," he said to the red haired woman with many freckles

"You guys on a rest day?" asked Jason.

"We were working on 'Retribution' ", Rose said.

"Yeah that's a really popular climb, you guys send it?" he asked, remembering the difficulties of the awkward corner with the thin crack that flares and tightens, and wondering if they had successfully completed the climb.

"More like it sent us, packin'," Kyle replied , with an agreeable nod from Rose.

"Oh well, you've got all winter,yes?" asked Jason.

"It may take all winter," replied Kyle, "What are you up to?"

"I thought Chiara came up here for a run," he said , " Have you seen her?"

"You know, a car like Chiara's pulled into the parking area early this morning, but it was just barely light enough to see, so I wasn't sure," Kyle said.

"Yeah and then who ever it was sat in the car for a minute, then left," Rose added,
she knew from past conversations that Chiara really didn't like the testosterone fueled climbing scene and that it was hard for women to break into, "if you see her though, I have
the chalk bag that I borrowed last time she was out here."

"Okay," Jason said, as he looked around the canyon, he saw a climber on the reddish sandstone wall about a quarter mile down. This was getting more confusing by the minute, he trusted Chiara, but he worried about her state of mind last night and in the last couple of months. "Well I came here to do some climbing so I think I'll head down to 'Boundaries'."

"You gonna solo it?" Kyle asked shading his eyes with his hand from the afternoon sun.

"Yeah, I've done it before ; I'm pretty solid on it ."

"Okay take it easy man," Kyle said as Jason walked back to his truck. He grabbed his equipment and headed down the trail.

He knew that solo climbing was controversial and somewhat on the edge even for experienced climbers. It was accepted as each climber's personnel choice. Most of the controversy came from the general public's ignorance and fear.

Jason embraced the practice because he experienced a graceful connection between his body and mind that only a successful solo climb delivered. It motivated him to search himself.

Climbers are encouraged and allowed to name the first ascent of a particular climb. They also give it a rating, indicating the difficulty. The 'Boundaries' climb was an aesthetically beautiful climb situated off the approach road; the entry was located on a side gully .

As rock climbing gained popularity and climbers conquered more rocks, there arose an additional personality theory labeled by psychologists as the type "T" personality. The T stands for thrill seekers or, as commonly referred to by climbers themselves, the 'adrenaline junkies'.

Jason theorized this personality trait was a genetic evolutionary inheritance that carried over from prehistoric days when hunters had to face off with mammoths and kill them to feed their families.

In modern times, though when the scariest part of getting food is slipping on a grape in the grocery aisle; and with not much call for mammoth meat, people have turned to voluntary doses of fear to quench the prehistoric longing?

The longing was paramount in Jason and manifested itself in many ways; primarily by climbing without any form of safety equipment . The line between controlling fear and succumbing to it often represented the very fine line between life and death.

A canyon wren song echoed downward into a spiraling sound that echoed low in thecanyon. He turned down the side trail and within two minutes could see the wall that called him.

The trail so steep that the approaching climber was in the unique position of looking down on the climb. The light tan sandstone wall splotched with rust colored patina. Patina is an armor plating that forms on the sandstone because of iron oxide in rain water. Sometimes it is extensive but in this case erosion had taken the majority of it off; giving the wall a speckled appearance.

Jason always felt himself sinking into a trance as he prepared for a solo climb; due in part to the solitude and because the task at hand required a calm and well focused approach. He sat down at the base of the wall and began the ritual in the way he always performed before a climb.

The first activity in the preparations included a stretch for his sore muscles. Next he slipped into the tight climbing shoes and laced them up firmly. Then he clipped his chalk bag around his waist and his Walkman to his belt.

The headphones slipped over his closely shorn head and he dipped his hands into the chalk bag which prevented them from sweating. The music began to play in his ears; it was a tape that Chiara had made.

The first song was the Rolling Stones classic 'Wild Horses'. Jason stopped what he was doing to take in the words.

The combination of a strumming acoustical guitar and the clean licks of an electric guitar set the mood for the lyrics:

> *"Tired of living, it's easy to do,*
> *I watched you suffer and go into pain,*
> *I know I dreamed you,*
> *I have my freedom but I don't have much time,*
> *Let's do some living after we die."*

The lyrics of the song took Jason back several months to think about Ciara's drop into the dark place that only she could know. He wasn't well versed in these problems; he always thought that he had done something wrong when she became sad and disinterested in activities that she always had enjoyed. Even her libido suffered.

And the most confusing thing for Jason was, other times when she was having a good day, Chiara could be so intensely passionate. Then the sex was wild and lasted a long time and left both of them spent and satisfied.

The greatest part of that Chiara was she liked to be in control which he was very unfamiliar with, since most of the women he had been intimate with would let the man take control. Then like throwing a light switch Chiara would drop into a place that Jason couldn't talk her out of.

He always thought he was in the 'doghouse' for some reason known only to her. They lived busy lives and sometimes were apart for long periods of time. Jason worried at times about other men but never had any proof and as quickly as Chiara would drop into these spells, she would pop out of them.

Right then and there Jason decided he would talk to Chiara about the emotional cycles and strive to get to the bottom of the problem. He didn't realize until just now, how much it bothered him. He leaned against the wall and felt cool stone on his face and against the palms of his hands. He breathed a deep sigh of release. He communed with the rock to feel the strength and power it contained; he yearned to draw it into his body.

The climb started with a couple petite holds, which led to a hefty, jug of a hold, merely fifteen feet above sandy ground at the base of the climb. However, after the jug the wall went blank for a five foot stretch of uninterrupted sandstone; followed by another large in-cut hold, the top of which welcomed the grasp of a human hand.

To bridge a stretch of smooth sandstone a climber must launch him or her self free of the wall and make a grab for the upper hold. The best climbers had perfected the exact amount of force needed to leap the smooth stone distance in such a way they neither rose past the hold, nor fell away from it. The point at very top of the leap is called the 'dead point'. Because you are neither rising or dropping, you are just frozen but only for a moment of time. If one fails to reach an exact place in space in which their body is weightless, the strain on their arms is too great. Hence the 'dead point'.

Only seasoned climbers' had great success achieving a dead point. The advantage of this technique is that they could float by a blank section of wall; not unlike the sensation of flowing over the top of a roller coaster hill, just before the plunge down over the other side.

CHAPTER 5

The tan lithe body lay stunned on the sand. Disbelief numbed her. For several minutes she re-lived the sliding, rolling, free falling. Shocking sensations waved across her body as each part of the fall flashed back to her mind, frame by frame; from the fish hook cactus to the ice cold water.

The slide and fall lasted only a few seconds and then the shock of the ice cold water on her hot sweaty body felt like an eternity only to suck the breath right out of her. Short lived relief washed over her on that sand; then a chilly realization came to her.

Something deep inside moved; not only the broken or badly bruised left ribs obvious with every breath, but the realization she could have died in two different ways; blunt force trauma and by drowning.

In a profound moment her soul sensed a shift that changed her forever. As the ragged pain coursed through her body she cringed; yet the sky never blossomed so crystal blue above her. The pain electrified everything in her body, but everything outside her pulsed with life and illumination.

She wiggled her fingers and determined normal sensation and ability. The body inventory revealed everything working within normal parameters and yet pain came from many different parts.

Chiara knew from medical experience that neck injuries are one of the biggest dangers of a fall. In fact, she had seen patients who had walked into the emergency department with serious spine injuries.

"Maybe I have a spinal injury that is making me see brighter colors?" she mumbled to herself as she ran her fingers down the back of her neck. No step offs, no point tenderness, she lifted her head and turned it from side to side, no pain. yet the grains of sand beneath her emitted a brighter hue of red than she had ever seen before, then she realized she was looking at her own blood.

Chiara attempted to lift her torso by pushing herself up with her arms until pain shot down her left side. Gritting her teeth, she pushed on the sand to roll over and sit up. The movement radiated the pain more intensely. Determined, she struggled to her right foot and she steadied herself against the side of the canyon.

A cold sweat slipped down her back as she looked around to get her bearings. The slot canyon ran just slightly off to an east, west alignment. It was still early so the sun hadn't reached the floor of the slot.

Upon standing, the cold sweat ramped into a complete body shiver.

She winced in pain as she took her first step to discover that she probably had strained her left ankle, or the tendons of the same leg. It was still early and she could take her time; crawl if necessary. She had to get back to her car; the sooner the better.

She glanced down at the goose bumps on her arm.

"These soaking wet clothes have to go." More pain accompanied the lifting action of her white and purple nylon tank top, followed by the gray jog bra; next came the wet running shorts. Injured ribs prevented fast or twisting movements, so carefully she draped the items on nearby rocks.

Now fully naked she assessed the abrasions accumulated on that slide. Her small breasts sloped down into uplifted brown areolas that circled pointy nipples; erect from the cold and without wounds. She looked down her left side to see red and purple abrasions from beneath her left breast to her thigh; the elbow and knee were also scraped. She drew a full breath to determine her lung function and found it painful but possible. Her ankle swelled and began to throb.

Her body, fit and trim had a classic rafter's tan even though she used sun block religiously. Jason and Chiara were both comfortable with nudity but in the presence of customers they had to be clothed. And the life jackets were always worn so the tan was mostly arms and legs. She brushed the clinging sand off her sore body. Each stroke of her arm accompanied pain that stole her breath. Within the hour a light breeze pulled most of the moisture from her runner's clothes. Still shivering she slipped them carefully back on.

Then Chiara shuffled into the sun and surveyed her location to further assess the level of her predicament.

The fall had placed her directly into a plunge pool that had broken her fall below the pour off. The layer of rock that had bounced her and had formed the pour off was more impenetrable than the rock under it.

"Probably limestone," she surmised. The soft underlying rock had eroded more submissively over the millennium. This formed a cap where the denser limestone hung out over the yielding sandstone under it.

"That hard limestone protects the sandstone," she said gazing at the undercut sandstone, "It's like what Jason alway's wants to do with me ," she whispered to the sky.   Fresh awareness trembled through her bruised body.

The shivering motivated her to move and begin the search for an exit to this canyon; it could be a long day. Limping down the slot, she found the main part of Bruja canyon was still up ahead. This was just a minor side slot canyon and it continued to drop in increments down to Bruja. Maybe this would lead her to the exit.

Chiara limped carefully on and after a turtle-slow fifty feet she reached the end of the slot canyon.

To her dismay she stood above another pour off onto the main floor of Bruja canyon. Crumbling down inside and out, she managed to inch forward on elbows and toes.

White zigzag lines raced through her brain and nausea rolled her stomach each time she moved the left side of her body, now swelling as protection to her traumatized ribs. The

hope of seeing another large plunge pool below this rim pushed her on. Her heart froze as she frantically scanned the canyon below.

Several large boulders splayed like a barely tapped rack of pool balls, to lay directly beneath the pour off rim; exactly where she would land. There was water in the pool but she assumed it only to be half way up the side of the boulders. The height of the jump would most certainly kill her when she hit the rocks; or even worse, the heart would continue to beat as every broken bone in her body pierced bloody tattered skin. In the nightmarish vision, she lay there throbbing ; forced to watch the carrion eaters from the sky circle and wait to taste her crimson blood. Her mind spun her belly into a dry heave.

The reality of the situation overwhelmed her ability to cope. Bruised body, spirit and soul approached complete shock.

Chiara had fallen into a slot canyon that was a perfect natural prison for humans and most animals.

The polished rock cap prevented a climb to safety. The rocks below prevented a leap to safety. Shear water polished smooth walls on both sides of the slot canyon prevented any hope of a handhold.

She curled into a fetal position at the edge of the final pour off. Tears flooded her cheeks; sobs rocked her body and soul. She wished the fall had killed her.

"I can't deal with this impossible situation! Not in this condition." Wails lulled into moans; exhaustion pushed Chiara further into dark whimpering sleep.

———————————

Some people would consider Jason suicidal, but he and others that participated in these activities believed living out on the edge, in the literal sense, was the only true life. Hc had contemplated this state of mind many times in the past and came to the conclusion that primitive peoples faced fearful situations on a daily basis. This essentially bathed their brains in a constant flow of adrenaline, resulting in tolerance and eventually addiction to the substance; possibly making the need for it, a permanent mark on the human genetic code.

This idea made perfect sense to Jason. He wondered theoretically speaking;
could it be possible the gene for risk-taking behavior surface in people at about the same frequency as green eyes for example?

His thoughts propelled him up the climb after the dead point but halfway up the route, fifty feet off the ground he became stumped.

The climb was familiar to him; he had been on it at least three times before, he found himself surprised by the impasse. He knew the answer was right there in front of him. Why couldn't he figure it out ? Thoughts of Chiara flew though his mind.

This climb was one of his favorites and he had done it successfully before and yet the thoughts of Chiara robbed his mind of the ability to focus and see the moves of the climb.

The sun pressed down full bore. Bruja canyon was in noon day light . Water gurgled and spun silver down the canyon providing a hypnotic sound. Birds floated and then raced both directions the length of the canyon. Their melodies called out to echo and soothe anything close enough to hear. Azure skies sliced red rock canyon walls above the prone and cramped human.

The downward spiraling calls of canyon wrens combined with the wind through the canyon created a hauntingly erie melody.

"So that's how this canyon got it's name," Chiara thought.

Chiara laid with eyes clenched tight; remembering the accident. She had slept for hours; lost in sadness. Each muscle and bone in her body told the story. Each tormented and dramatic second flooded through her again and she embraced the sand under her to stop the rolling of her mind and her stomach. Then the fully out of control plunge into icy water caused her stomach muscles to clench, momentarily paralyzing her diaphragm. The memory sucked the breath out of her. Lying in the sand she wished she was embracing Jason during this time of fear and sadness.

She wondered what Jason was doing right now. He is a very stable man but was he pulling his hair out with worry. Will he come and rescue me?

"STOP!" she shouted to herself. She couldn't keep waiting for a knight in shinning armor. She would have to figure out how to get out of this.

It was warm now. The scent of water and earth filled her nostrils. Her mind re-surfaced to a quiet place, full of peace and nature filled sounds.

Inhaling as deeply as she could manage; she mentally captured control and purposely tensed her pain once more, embracing and exploring it. Holding for seconds, she exhaled slow and then coolly willed herself into a release of the pain and the memories. She mentally nudged her body to lie deeply and fully relaxed against the warm nurturing sand.

When she moved a full five minutes later to sit up the road rash road rash tightened on the left side of her body. Time and meditation had stabilized the wound and allowed her a precise evaluation of the pros and cons; they felt manageable . Determined to escape this nightmare, she looked once more toward the pour off.

From her sitting perspective, she tried to calculate how much speed it would take to clear the boulders and land in the soft sand beyond. The distance she would have to cover to propel her body to safety was ten maybe fifteen feet.

"That distance may be possible on a flat and manicured track and in perfect health." she muttered to herself. But the canyon floor was uneven and her ankle would prevent her from getting any speed. Just jumping off the edge would put her dead center in the middle of the boulders.

The last move Jason had made on the deadpoint was difficult enough he didn't want to try to down climb. The golden rule of the solo climber had been broken-- never climb up anything you can't down climb.

'What was I thinking?" he said under his labored breath.

Instead, he moved into a repetitive sequence of holding on with one hand while shaking out the other arm and chalking that hand. From past experience he knew that this was a terminal technique that would eventually run it's course, because his tired fingers could melt off the holds and he would become another statistic.

Immediately, he forced himself to purge any distracting thoughts; but this whole thing with Chiara kept cropping up. "Damn her anyway! For not letting me know where she went, then going there!" he growled. Then he inhaled deeply, his anger was misdirected, it wasn't Chiara's fault that he chose to solo today.

He made great effort to maintain control and keep fear and panic from taking charge, causing him to lose flow and focus. A powerful struggle surged within him. Tendons corded, lean muscles tensed toward knotting, as he hung suspended in the pre-violence of a fall;

memories flashed. And in that split second; illumination flushed up his spine as Chiara's face flooded his mind.

"Until you commit fully to something you can't fully understand it or yourself." A friend's voice whispered through him.

Solo climbing is all about identifying, respecting and honoring your limitations.

With those thoughts guiding him, Jason slid his fingers under a hold and moved his feet up as high as he could. Choosing to take the chance that if his grip wavered he could never recover from the fall.

The risk paid off. Placing his feet higher allowed him to push past the difficulties, reach the next large hold and move on to complete the climb.

The 'zone', as it is most commonly called by the rock climbers and other athletes is a mental state in which they often find themselves. This place is achieved by the person that has developed a repetitive cycle of physical and mental actions that, when learned by the muscles, tendons and nerves, eventually happens automatically when the same set of circumstances align; thus a higher level of achievement is allowed; one that moves the athlete from novice to professional in every sport.

Only when the zone is achieved effortlessly by the person through consistent practice, can the state of mind connect so perfectly with the body's kinetics memory that precise physical activity can occur without the interference of the mind.

The zone served Jason well throughout his climbing career. In that meditative state, his problematic situations resolved and enlightened moments of solution often surfaced.

At the top of the cliff he rested to savor the victory over fear and his own mind. The feeling of success over possible death lightened and floated him across the sky.

Time moved around him like water silently and effortlessly slipped around a mid- stream boulder. A slight breeze engulfed and warmed him as mind and body relaxed down from the adrenaline bath.

He had planned to do at least one more climb this day, but the one just completed drained him of the need, and seemed sacred somehow; a good place to stop. It was as close as he had come to an out of body experience. His body satisfied; his mind calmed into and flowed into a working solution for his relationship with Chiara.

This juncture in space was crystal clear to Jason; rocks vibrated into deeper hued colors, bird songs were profound melodies in perfect cadence to his heartbeat; the love he felt for Chiara pulsed and echoed into his soul. Life shimmered around and through him and fresh awareness washed over him. The face of the woman of his dreams floated before him, beside him.

Slipping on his sandals, he walked back to the trail on the top of the cliff. He paused in search of a sensation of Chiara's presence.

"Where are you Chi?"

Nothing came to him. he squatted to move his face closer to the ground in an attempt to see, see or feel a track or some tiny scuff she may have left indicating she had been on the trail. His spirit willed anything that would point out her passing to come to him; now. Straining his eyes, heart and mind saw only ground hard packed and pressed that revealed nothing.

An urgent sense of Chiara's danger pressed against him to steal his breath away and stand the hair at the back of his neck on end.

Not prone to panic, an abrupt and desperate urge to find her swallowed him.

Chiara looked up and down the main canyon. The slight turns in both directions could be seen about a quarter of a mile away. To her right, down in the canyon there was actually another drop into the main floor of Bruja. It was called 'The Keyhole'. Jason had taken her there one day while they were climbing up from the mouth of the canyon.

He explained the Keyhole was formed when a large boulder became wedged at the lip of the pour off. Over the years, floods brought gravel and debris down to fill in around the base of the boulder, but a hole remained to drain the flood waters.

This particular hole was just large enough for the shoulders of the average person to pass through; hence the name 'The Keyhole'. People descending the canyon could wriggle through the keyhole, cutting out miles of walking to the mouth of the canyon.

"Voices?" Suddenly Chiara froze.

She listened again, but couldn't be sure.

"Heelllppp!" she screamed.

"Help," echoed back.

She listened long, but only silence slithered back to her.

"Heellp!" Her voice pleaded. Hands cupped around her mouth to yell up canyon, down canyon, then she howled straight up into the endless blue. A primal scream tore from her lonely soul.

For the next two hours she pleaded with the sky, the sand and the rocks that someone would hear and realize she was in danger. No human sound returned.

Despondent, she limped back up the slot canyon to the water hole that saved her life before she sat on the sand.

"This precious water," sighed out of her in a whisper.

"It could be worse. At least I won't die an agonizing death of thirst." She stared into the calm pool beneath her reflection.

One swollen cloud pushed her face aside in the water-mirror. Looking up she shivered. The sight of a brooding and blooming cloud, know as a thunderhead sunk into her. She turned over and looked up at the sky to see an imposing stratocumulus cloud taking up the majority of the sky.

"Great! Now I will be pummeled by more water falling from the sky." Gloom surrounded her. She slumped against the canyon wall, giving way again to the weight of it all.

Bruised muscles and joints throbbed in pain. Her throat raw from the screaming; the situation saturated her like a dark wet blanket.

"Why do I worry about hydration or staying dry?" she thought . I am going to die in this canyon; or on the escape attempt from this prison." Tears seeped from her eyes; a silent testimony cried her into mentally exhausted sleep.

Several hours later she jerked awake with a quick shudder. The temperature had dropped precisely with the sun as it began the slip below unseen horizons. Desert air experiences a wide range of temperatures between sunrise and sunset.

Thin running clothes were not enough for warmth. A groan escaped Chiara's lips as daylight faded into purple twilight then the total black of night; the realization of surviving the first night with a twisted ankle, very little food and even less cover trembled through her. To prevent hypothermia she spent the rest of the night doing intermittent and partial push ups, sit-ups and squats; as allowed by her injuries. At this juncture, she functioned at about forty percent on all levels.

Thousands of stars pierced the tiny wedged piece of sky directly above her. Bats fluttered down into the main canyon, she could see their silhouetted shapes against the stars. Coyotes made mournful calls to other members of their pack. The night seemed endless as bouts of shivering shook her to the core. She had heard that death from hypothermia was very peaceful and that people actually felt warm just before death took them.

She knew she had to keep awake during the night for two reasons; to endure the cold, and because sound traveled better in low dew-point night air. She might be able to hear human activity at a greater distance. But it was a truly silent night.

Finally the eastern horizon flushed ever so slightly; two hours later dawn broke and an hour after that; strong sunlight reached down to stroke the slot canyon. Chiara collapsed in relief and exhaustion as the sun massaged her skin, muscle and bone.

"I feel ready to die now." Instead sleep drifted into the dream of strong caring arms holding her close.

CHAPTER 6

The traffic back to Littlefield was light and Jason drove like a lunatic but it was still ten minutes after five when he pulled into town. He slowed to pass the triangle intersection and nodded to the elderly woman who seemed to be scolding him; or someone unseen. Jason swung the red pickup into the yellow gravel lot and his disposition immediately nose-dived; Chiara's car was not at the house. Steg started welcoming, whinning, and scolding all at the same time.

"It wasn't 'THAT' long. How are ya man?" he consoled the cat quickly so he could look around the house. The note on the kitchen table appeared to be untouched. And he hit the table out of a frustration that was becoming more and more scary.

He could make some phone calls and see if she was anyplace nearby or had changed her plans, or drive through town to see if she was at the grocery store, but he didn't want to sound the alarm just yet; it wasn't even dark.

Jason flopped down on the old ragged couch that had come with the house and stroked Steg, now in a state of half-lidded ecstasy. He created and rehearsed the words he would use to bring up the conversation about their relationship.

After awhile, Jason began to pace back and forth in the living room. He hated this lack of control feeling. He peered out of the front window and noticed the dusk creeping in to surround the town of Littlefeild. The elderly woman lingered in the highway triangle.

Within a minute of his watching, a middle aged man, balding on top and graying around the sides, walked toward the woman and into the triangle. He talked to her for a minute, and then offered his hand. Eventually, she reached out to him, They walked back down the road into town; the woman talking and gesturing all the way. This scene mildly surprised Jason but his mind was working overtime on other concerns.

The anxiety and unease about Chiara were beginning to wear on him. He didn't have any hard facts but he sensed trouble. He needed to do something to bring relief to these feelings. Jason placed a call to Mesquite Emergency Department.

"Mesquite Memorial, Molly speaking."

"Hi Molly,is Chiara working tonight?"

"No she's not", then as an after thought, "Whose calling please?'

"This is Jason, I'm not sure we've met Molly, but I'm her boyfriend. She went for a run today and should have been home hours ago."

"Oh.No, she's not scheduled to work 'til Saturday."

"Okay, I thought she may have picked up another shift."

"Not today Jason."

"Okay, thanks Molly."

He put a finger on the disconnect button and the phone clicked off. Then without replacing the receiver, he dialed 911.

"Llittlefield Police Department . What's your emergency?"

"Umm, I'm just wondering if you've had any reports of car accidents involving a faded yellow Subaru?"

"No, are you witnessing an accident, sir?" the dispatcher asked.

"No, my girlfriend is late getting home, and I just thought I'd check."

"Uh, no. No accidents."

"Thanks for your help."

Jason hung up but wasn't sure what to do at this point. With a sigh he stepped out into warm, dark air and tired to organize his thoughts. Should he just go to sleep and maybe Chiara would be here by morning? Maybe sleep would help him reduce his anxiety.

How could he go to sleep knowing she might be hurt or lost or....? The cat rubbed his leg and cried out for attention.

"Don't panic Steg! She might have decided to spend the night on a big rock, thinking.

He laughed to himself and realized that sleep would be a miracle tonight with his mind working every angle.

"Back later Steg. Hold down the fort."

He stepped into the cab of his red pickup and simply sat there for a couple minutes.

Chiara wouldn't leave him without a word, sure things had become a little rocky over the last few months but Chiara was all about communication. Suddenly Jason jumped as a dark movement flashed into his peripheral vision. Yellow eyes glistened through the windshield and a soft tentative meow spoke to him.

Jason chuckled as his heart rate pounded in the carotid arteries of his neck. He started the truck and Steg jumped down to run off into the night. He drove thirty minutes to La Kiva Bar and Grill; a classic hang out for climbers and outdoor buffs in the area.

La Kiva was one of the more unique structures Jason had ever seen. He walked up to the monolithic front door made from five burly railroad ties that leaned at a sharp angle against the building. The door was secured with heavy duty steel hinges and had a steel handle. The monster door tipped the scales at more than five hundred pounds.

A cable attached to the upper left corner of the door ran through a huge rusted pulley and allowed mere mortals to open this vault. Four hundred and ninety five pounds of scrap steel hung from the end of the cable. The weight of the steel counter-balanced the weight of the door which could swing easily with five pounds of pull.

Jason walked inside and nodded to a couple raft guides sitting at the bar. Then he moved up to the bar.

The bartender was fifty year old man with a weighty belly, gray hair and white beard. Tattoos festooned big arms crossed over a barrel chest and rested atop his ponderous gut. He didn't speak but made eye contact and nodded his head. His pocked and pitted complexion might have contained knife scars, but in the low light it was hard to tell.

"I'll have a Beck's dark."

The bartender opened a glass refrigerator door, pulled out the green bottle of beer, popped the top under the bar and handed it to Jason.

"Three fifty," the bartender said with a croaky voice.

Jason pulled a five from his pocket and handed it to the toad like man. He returned with a dollar and two quarters.

"Need a glass?" he asked .

"No. I'm good," Jason replied with a slight wave of his hand.

He walked to a booth, slid in across a polished bench, took a pull off his bottle and gazed around the bar.

The interior was no less amazing than the door. The floor was recessed into the ground and large beams led up in a spoke-like manner to a ring of unknown material in the center of the room.

Hanging from the walls and ceiling beams in what seemed like organized clutter were long horn cow skulls, rattlesnake skins, even an aborigine didgoridoo, which was a musical instrument of Australian Aborigines.

There were literally thousands of pieces from the desert environs. The ceiling was painted black to match the black tile of the floor; the room instigated the feeling of floating in space. Jason drifted into a trance-like stare while his mind imagined a number of terrible events.

"Dude!" Jason jerked in his seat; standing beside him was Tommy Perkins.

"How long have you been standing there?" Jason stammered trying yo recover from the shock.

"I walked in the door, across the floor, and right up to your table about thirty seconds ago." Tommy said grinning widely. "You were sitting here like a zombie."

"How did you know I was here?"

"I didn't but I was headed home from work and saw your truck." Tommy said, "Let me grab a beer."

Tommy returned from the bar with his beer and slid into the booth across from Jason.

"Now why are you sitting here staring into space?' Tommy asked.

"Chiara went for a run this morning before dawn and hasn't come home yet."

"Is that unusual?"

"She usually doesn't run for fourteen hours straight. I have this funny feeling something is wrong."

"Well Chiara is a pretty tough cookie. She can handle herself." Tommy said as he took a drink from his beer.

"How do you know she went for a run?"

"She left me a note this morning that she was going to do the upper Gorge trail," Jason said taking another drink.

"Have you looked for her?"

"Yeah. I went down to the Gorge and talked to Kyle and Rose, who said they thought they had seen her car this morning but no one got out and it drove away."

"How weird is that?" Tommy said, running his hand through his black curly hair. "Did you climb?"

"Yeah I soloed Boundaries."

"You're nuts, man!"

"Yeah especially since I almost cratered," Jason said, "But that's not important now, I'm just trying to decide what to do about Chiara."

"What have you done so far?"

"I called the hospital. She's not working nor is she a patient. I called the cops; no reported accidents, I'd go out looking for her, but I don't know where she is for sure."

Tommy just sat there shaking his head and all he could say was, "Wow."

"I think I should go home and if she's not there, I'll call the cops, and report her missing."

"I'm with ya there."

Jason and Tommy finished their beers and tried to think of other possibilities. The bar was near empty and quiet. It did a respectable business from Thursday to Sunday but on Monday, this evening, patrons were scarce.

"Well if you need help with anything, I'll be glad to help."

"Not, tonight. Think I'll head home and call the cops."

"Okay, man call if you need anything, this is freaky."

The men left La Kiva and drove in opposite directions.

CHAPTER 7

The midnight black hummer rolled out of the underground garage. This normally locked building was used for Scapalini family business only. Jack was at the wheel, with Joey in the back seat holding court. To his right in the front seat sat Vinny Scapalini, Joey's younger brother. Jack loathed Vinny even more than most people.

Vinny Scapalini was the scourge of Mesquite, Nevada. He followed Joey and the rest of the family to Nevada from Atlantic City, New Jersey about a year after Joey became established here. The truth was he was chased out. When asked he was eager to provide the story of how he was forced to leave the east coast to avoid prison for all the people he had killed.But since there were no extradition orders everyone saw through that story. He was nothing but a bully; inflicting pain and suffering on weaker people to stroke his ego. Joey took pity on him because he was family and with all the threats around the family, they had to stick together.

Joey gave Vinny the title 'Head of Security' , for the Crown Jewels Casino, but every one knew it was a title with no punch and also knew who held the real title. However, the reputation that Vinny had created for himself back east added some power to the Scapalini Family influence in the small town of Mesquite. Even though Joey bent over backwards to separate himself from any criminal past and to establish a legitimate enterprise; town folk feared the family from the East Coast because of all the rumors that had accompanied them.

Jack usually liked driving the Hummer because it felt like driving a street legal tank. The Hummer was the civilian version of the HumVee and joey snapped one up as soon as they were offered.

This trip started out as a punishment for Jack because the passenger beside him was in Jack's estimation , one of the lowest forms of human kind. Vinny had tortured animals as a kid. Now, physically much bigger and more powerful; he picked fights he knew he could win and ran from fights that he was sure to lose. Jack hated Vinny but there wasn't much he could do about it with Joey being his brother and running the show, and now riding in the back seat.

His little brother was a lot of work for Joey because he constantly found trouble with the law, and the last thing the family needed was more scrutiny from local law enforcement . The latest issue with Vinny was a show girl that refused his advances and received Vinny's unbridled anger. Vinny spent the night in jail but was released the next day. Three months later Jack saw the dancer driving a brand new Corvette and rumor had it that she had dropped against Vinny.

The bully's squinty eyes gazed out the windshield, a sour expression on his face. He pouted because Joey dragged him out of bed earlier than he wanted after spending a night out partying. Joey was doing some legal paperwork in the back seat.

"Rough night there Vinny?" Jack teased, with a grin on his face.

Vinny turned his head to looked Jack through swollen eyes. A bump in the highway caused his double chins to bounce.

"I told you, my name is Vincent. I'm trying to drop the mafia image, okay G.I. Joe," Vinny growled. The disdain obviously went in both directions.

"Well maybe you should stop beatin' up chicks," Jack retorted.

"One of these days I'm going to break your fingers and then your neck." Vinny sneered.

"Shut up Vinny," Joey chided from the back seat.

Vinny lit a cigarette and continued pouting.

The highway crossed into a corner of Arizona and then wound back north into Utah. After an hour of driving , the Hummer exited the highway and headed west into the town of St. George. The drive had been tense and silent. Driving through St. George the Hummer turned every head on the street. They continued west towards the Mormon Mountains. Vinny slept in the passenger seat with his obese face pressed against the window; drool drained from his mouth down his chin and slimed the glass.

Joey broke the silence. "Jack, tell me about this guy Joseph Rains."

"First of all, he goes by the nick name Rake," said Jack carefully trying to avoid the verbal play he had with Joey the last time they discussed Joseph Rains.

"Rake Rains?" Joey asked "Is he a garden tool or a man?"

"I don't know sir." Jack replied knowing full well that Joey had never had a garden tool in his hand.

"What do you know about him?" Joey asked .

"He used to be a hard core Mormon; you know the kind with ten wives and a hundred kids," Jack said. "About fifteen years ago he was busted by the church and the state as an example to other of those types, now hiding out in the deserts of Utah."

"Yeah, what are those people called?" Joey asked .

"Polygamists," Jack answered.

"I call'em stupid. I can barely stand one wife and three kids," Joey laughed.

Jack smiled and nodded his head.

"Go on Jack."

"When he was released from prison, he was a changed man."

"What do you mean?"

"When he went to prison another guy moved in and took over his harem like an alpha male taking over a pack," Jack said. "Half of them went off and found other men."

Jack stopped and pulled out an atlas to find a dirt road running off the main road ; the turn off was still five miles further on.

"When did he get out of the slammer?"

"About seven years ago, but he didn't go looking for his women or kids. Instead, he became a recluse and moved into a shack on the back acres of his property, where nobody really bothers him."

"He lives there alone?' Joey asked.

"Far as I know."

Jack found the dirt side road and turned right; headed for the distant mountains. The road ran past several ranches surrounded by herds of cattle and horses.

"Will he sell the canyon to us?"

"I don't know, it may be a hard sell, he's probably pissed off at the world."

"Maybe money will make him friendlier."

"Maybe he's dirt poor ," Jack responded.

"Well here's a question for you Jack, how the hell are we going to get the water to Mesquite. We have been driving for almost an hour?"

"Driving here takes an hour because there is no road over the mountains."

"But?"

"But we are less than ten miles from Mesquite, as the crow flies, we've actually crossed over the Nevada state line about a minute ago."

"You are a fricking genius Jack!"

"Thank you sir."

The three pulled into a gas station and Jack filled up the tank while Joey and Vinny walked into the convenience store. A group of people gathered near the hummer, but at a respectable. distance, to check out the latest high priced boy toy from Detroit. The gas station's attendant spoke to Joey, admiring the vehicle and heaping compliments on the design for it's ultimate off-road image as promoted in magazines.
Joey pulled out a hundred dollar bill to pay for the gas and a pack of cigarettes for Vinny. Then the three climbed back into the vehicle and Jack pulled out of the gas station.

The Hummer raised a high dust plume behind it. A couple miles in the distance an impressive escarpment rose straight up out of the desert. Three ramshackle buildings with corrugated sheet metal roofs hunkered low up against the cliff; as if backed into a corner by the world. The buildings were surrounded by welded steel corrals. A couple bone weary horses swatted flies inside one of the pens and an assortment of rusted, broken down vehicles were scattered throughout the buildings.

A man, wearing faded blue overalls and a dirty white tee shirt leaned over the engine compartment of a fifty-seven Chevy pickup that only a mechanic could love.

As the Hummer drew closer to the corral the men could see 'No Trespassing' signs. The man under the hood of the pickup turned, looked at the approaching vehicle and then quickly walked into another building that served as a house. Simultaneously, two dogs rose from the shade of the house and made a bee line out to the Hummer.

Both the reddish tan dogs were wide in the shoulders, round in the face and had a line of near black hair growing the wrong direction down their spines. This trait is commonly found in the lion killing hounds bred in Africa known by the name Rhodesian Ridgebacks. The reverse hairs stood vertically to indicate an agitated state right before they attacked. The hairs stiffened as the dogs barked and snarled at the tires of the vehicle.

Belligerent animal sounds startled Vinny awake; he immediately reached for his pistol but Joey jerked forward over the seat-back to grab Vinny's gun.

"Take it easy, I don't want to kill this guy's dogs or he'll never talk to us," Joey said.

Vinny, recoiled in his seat and leaned back from the window to watch the dogs through the bullet proof glass. The animals, catching scent of his fear, leapt up to snarl and bite at bugged out Vinny eyes. Strings of dog saliva streaked parallel to his recent spittle.

"Let me shoot the son's-of-bitches!" Vinny growled back in a low voice.

Jack brought the vehicle to a quick stop by the corral; hopped out of the driver's seat and sank down on one knee near the vehicle door. Vinny's mouth gaped open, as he and Joey watched with surprise and interest.

Spurred by the opening of the car door, the dogs bolted around the Hummer. Jack met them with his extended left hand, palm down. His eyes averted, the dogs stopped squared off with him on their level. His right hand rested on the Glock pistol beneath his jacket, just in case. He forced the air out of his lungs along with the tension out of his body and braced himself for the pain of canines sinking into his hand.

The dogs never ceased barking or snarling as they waited for the fear smell or some other subtle cue from this intruder that would stimulate the attack. After thirty seconds of stalemate, the dogs lowered their tails slightly, but continued the low growling; never taking their eyes off the intruder.

"Mr. Rains can we talk to you for a moment ?" Jack said in a calm but firm voice.

From the house a booming voice yelled, "Mack, Sally, back!" The dogs dropped their heads and tails, then started to move away whinning and whimpering. A barrel- chested man strode across the corral with six shot revolver nestled into his belt.

A spasm of relief flooded through Jack as sweat beads trickled into his eyes and out from under his arms. But he still showed no emotion. His hunch had played out.

The sun-wrinkled, wind worn man approached stiffly. He drew near, then stood tall with his legs spread; one just in front of the other.

The adrenaline washed out of Jack's veins and his pulse slowed. "This guy means business, but doesn't want trouble, just wants to be left alone." he thought.

Rake Rains was a stocky man with gray hair and a gray beard that had been recently shaped with the exception of a few stragglers indicating a self-inflicted trim. Ruddy skin hung on high cheek bones to wrinkle around intense blue eyes accustomed to watching on far horizons. A combination of engine grease and desert dust covered him from grizzled face to well worn overalls. A nothing-to-lose attitude was emitting from him. He had stopped six feet from the corral fence.

As the dust settled, Joey stepped out of the back seat of the Hummer which caused renewed growling from the dogs.

Rake responded, "Down." The dogs settled at his feet, their bodies between him and the strangers. Jack had noticed that there was a difference in personality between the dogs. The female was a lot less aggressive than the male, who seemed to want to eviscerate anything that moved.

Joey walked up beside Jack. Vinny sat frozen in his seat and the dogs continued to give low intermittent growls.

Rake locked his gaze on Jack and said. "Are you crazy mister?"

"No sir Mr. Rains. I meant you nor your animals no disrespect."

"That was a foolish move," Rake said, perturbed that his first line of defense had been defeated. "The animals could rip you're guts out before you stop breathing. Some people just don't got a lick of sense," he said shaking his head. Jack stood and listened to the scolding; perceptive that Rake was just trying to do damage control. Jack understood the dogs were important to his security, and he wanted Mr. Rains to feel secure so he could talk to him about the canyon.

"I've always admired Ridgebacks, Mr. Rains."

"They are Rhodesian Ridgebacks and Pit Bull mix; this can be a wild land with wild people wandering around it,"Rake replied.

"We understand sir."

"Speaking of that, what do you boys need? Run out of gas or something' ", then a sudden change came over Rake, the gun came up to a more ready position, and the dogs alerted to their master's tension, " Are you guys Feds?"

"No Sir," Jack said showing the rancher his hands.

"Mr. Rains my name is Joseph Scapalini, and I represent a land trust that would like to preserve Bruja Canyon for all eternity."

"What the hell is a land trust, Mister?"

"It is a group of investors that would buy the canyon from you, should you decide to sell, and then promise to always preserve it so that it can't be developed; you know , chopped up into little pieces." Joey answered.

"I'm doing a fine job taking care of this land myself. Trust me not that many people will face off with these dogs like your partner there," Rake said.

"I understand Mr. Rains, but you aren't a young man anymore and as you said it's a wild land out there and if something happened to you," Joey said as the old man scanned the Hummer and the suits. Sensing distrust in Rake he added, "We are not associated with the state or federal government in any way. We are a group of private investors."

Rake pondered the thought for a few moments as he looked from Joey to Jack and back to the black Hummer. Joey was dressed in a black suit with a black turtleneck and Jack much the same.

"You boys don't look like the the outdoor types that do a lot of hiking around here."

"Sir to accomplish this we have to raise a lot of money, that's our job; to raise money money and to protect this land for hikers," Jack said.

"That's a serious vehicle you got there, how much did that run you?" Rake asked .

"We spend a lot of time in the back country and we need a vehicle that can go there," Jack said, hoping that Rake wouldn't be up on the latest models coming out of Detroit.

"I'm gonna have to spend time thinking about this," Rake said with a completely non- expressive face; his arms crossed over his chest. "Why don't you check back with me in a couple weeks?"

"One more thing sir, you could become very wealthy from this transaction," Joey said trying to end the discussion with the ball in his court.

"How much you city slickers want to pay me?"

"One million dollars over ten years ," Joey said testing the depths of his greed.

"Huh?" Rake said, taken a little taken back by such a quick offer.

"We'd like to think of it as an investment in the future of your land," Joey said "We'll be in touch sir."

Rake watched with squinted eyes, trying to decide what to make of them as the men climbed back into the Hummer and drove away.

CHAPTER 8

Detective Robert Jones walked to the front door of the adobe structure; the black cat sitting on the porch turned and dashed into the desert. RJ as he was know to friends and co-workers, raised his hand to knock just as the door jerked open. Jason had been waiting anxiously for this visit.

"Hi, I'm Detective Jones from the Flagstaff office of the Arizona State Police." he said holding his badge up for Jason to see.

"I'm Jason I made the report last night."

"We got the report from the Littlefcild Police Department. We often help the smaller departments around the state with investigations." He waited for Jason to invite him in.

"Can I come in?" RJ asked.

"Of course, come in," Jason responded.

"I wasn't sure I'd get any help with this today. The cop that took the report last night said they couldn't put out an ABP for twenty four hours." Jason said as he felt a wave of relief flowing over him like a wave. It seemed he had done the right thing and now something was beginning to happen.

"Twenty four hours after last seen ," The detective said looking at the documents in his hand, "your statement said she was last seen yesterday morning."

"Yes that's right officer, I mean detective, " Jason said.

"Okay, just start from the beginning."

Jason related the story from the day before. There wasn't much to tell, she didn't come home. The cop watched every mannerism as Jason related the details of his story; the direction of his gaze, the tension in his fingers and how he moved his hands and his neck to see if the pulse was visible as it would be on a racing heart.

Jason felt the cop's scrutiny. His voice wavered a time or two. This was his first attempt to deliver details for a police report and he was afraid he would leave something out. The presence of the state police also indicated the event had elevated to the next level; crossing state crossing state lines had added implications.

RJ looked over the note Chiara had left, "Is there anything else you can tell me?" he asked.

"Like what?" Jason asked suddenly in a defensive mode.

"Did she have any enemies? How is your relationship? Is there any reason she would want to leave?"

"Well, we've been together of over a year. And we've had our tough times, like any couple, but nothing serious. We always figure things out."

"Can you tell me what she was wearing? And I'll need a description of her car."

Jason spent the next five minutes providing the information.

"Would you mind if I had a look around?"

"No, go ahead."

The detective wandered slowly through the house, looking through cabinets and poking around items in the dresser in the bedroom.

"Well I think I'm done here for now," RJ said.

"We'll put out an APB on her and the vehicle. But I have to tell you Jason, thousands of people go missing in this country every year. People getting away from their lives; some people have psychological problems and just wander off, and yes on occasion illegal abductions. But of those thousands of missing people only a small percentage are found."

Jason digested that bit of information and the thought came to his mind that he may never see Chiara again. He felt a lump forming in his throat and he shallowed so deeply even RJ heard it. With the many risk taking activities he had tackled in his life he was able to hold any panic down, at least for now.

"Oh and one more question before I go, who is the woman directing traffic out in front of this place. Jason's thoughts were far away from what he considered to be a pointless distraction. He shook his head to get together and focused. As both men gazed out the window Jason said, "We've been here for two month's and she's been out there every day, talking to herself and gesturing I don't know her name, but I saw a middle-aged man walking hand and hand with her back to town.

"Interesting," RJ said, then turned to go, extending a hand. Jason shook hands with him as RJ made a mental note that Jason's hands were dry, rough and very strong. "I'll be in touch with you regardless of where this goes. Call me at this number any time of the night or day if you think of something else, or if anything changes." The detective handed him a card then walked through the door and left in the unmarked car.

RJ drove across the lot and scrutinized the woman in the highway intersection triangle. He parked the car on the side of the road and walked across to the woman in the triangle.

She became silent and her eye lids lowered as she watched RJ approach. When he pulled out the badge in preparation for an introduction, the flash of it crinkled her face into a sneer. Before he could speak the woman unleashed a tirade.

"I've seen you before!" she growled, pointing at him with a crooked finger. "Don't come any closer to me. I know you're with the agency! What happened in Germany was a long time ago. Why don't you leave me alone?" she whined. The fierce look on her face revealed clues about her mental state. But despite her outward look of anger, she felt fear and uncertainty. Her eyes shifted as the severe look softened into regret. Then her voice changed up into a guilty pitch.

"It wasn't my fault! I know the dog died. I was watching it but it ran away," she said, her eyes looked through him rather than at him.

RJ understood he was dealing with a psychiatric problem as she talked non-stop. He finally squeezed out a word,"Ma'am?"

He had a black bag, he was hiding something, why won't you listen to me?" she blurted out.

"Who had a black bag, ma'am?" RJ tried to focus the woman. This detail sounded intriguing.

Before he could ask again, a vehicle pulled into the triangle and a balding middle aged man stepped out. RJ turned to look at him. The man had a cheek full of chewing tobacco which caused him to slur his words.

"Howdy there," the man said spitting on the ground.

"Hello I'm Detective Jones with the Arizona State Police. Do you know this woman?"

"My mother," the man said, "Did she break some law?"

"Not that I know of; I just wanted to ask her a few questions," he responded.

"Good luck," he chuckled, "she hasn't uttered a sensible word in the last ten years."

"Pardon me?"

"Schizophrenia; she started getting sick about fifteen years ago after my father left."

RJ stared at him, dumbfounded. This is gonna' be one of 'those' cases, he thought.

"Then she got meningitis and she has't been right since, "Tobacco man sprayed tobacco juice as he said the medical terms. I had her at the state hospital for a while but I couldn't afford it no more."

"Aren't you afraid she'll wander off? RJ asked.

"Oh. I own the gas station on the corner, over there. I can watch her every move. She never leaves this triangle; never hurts anybody."

RJ pondered this scene for a moment then said "Can you ask her some questions for me?"

"Sure, what's going on?"

"The woman who lives in this house," he pointed to the house, "has disappeared and I thought your mom may have seen something."

"Chiara?!" the man asked in a surprised tone . "Those two are such nice kids."

"Yeah," RJ returned, " have you noticed anything unusual. over there?"

"No.I haven't seen her for a couple days."

"I told you! Why don't you ever listen to me ?" the woman sputtered out in the direction of the men.

"Told me what?" RJ asked.

"It wasn't my fault the dog died! It ran away from me!" She stammered, eyes bulging in RJ's direction.

"We've never really figured out that story. Musta been childhood trauma," the son said.

RJ nodded as he spoke, and then thanked them for their help. He wandered the small town for the next few hours interviewing several people. Most people didn't know the couple had moved in two months ago.

As the white Crown Victoria with state plates pulled into the parking area of the gorge, the butt end of a marijuana-joint found it's way into the smoldering fire. The climbers pretended to be busy with other activities around the campsite. RJ stepped out of his car and walked over to the climbers. His corduroy blazer and khaki slacks looked out-of-place among the collection of grungy pants and fleece jackets. He flashed his badge and introduced himself. Then he explained the reason for his visit. Kyle and Rose stepped forward to speak with him.

"So you talked with Jason here yesterday afternoon?" RJ asked.

"Yeah, he was here looking for Chiara and he wanted to do a climb," Kyle said.

"Did you see him climbing?" RJ asked .

"No, but this is a big place, you could lose yourself back in here for a month."

"Or lose a body back here forever," RJ thought to himself.

" And how did he seem to you?"

"He was worried about Chiara but it was still early so he just thought it was a mistake and that she would show up pretty soon," Rose said.

"Have you ever seen problems between them; you know fights, etc."

"Sure everyone has their disagreements," she said. Then after a slight hesitation, offered, "Chiara was often sad, I've seen her crying on a few occasions and then at times she was so happy."

"Well now I have two options on this disappearance, murder and suicide," RJ thought.

"Where did you see the car that you thought was Chiara's?" RJ asked.

"Over there at the end of the parking area," Kyle pointed.

"Could you tell if there were one or more people sitting in the car?"

"No, too dark," Kyle said

"Okay, thanks ," RJ said and walked over to the car spot and looked down at the ground, There were definite tire tracks from an automobile but the sand was so loose nothing definite could be detected. His eyes raised to focus on the distance surrounding the car. He scanned the area. He imagined himself in the time and place when the girl in the yellow Subaru arrived. In his mind's eye he saw the car pull up and stop. Next, he put himself into the occupant's place.

CHAPTER 9

Jason stared at the phone and then, intermittently stood up and walked around the room; back and forth, no destination in mind. Finally he picked up the phone and dialed a phone number in Los Angeles, California.

He had spoken with Chiara's mother twice before when she had called looking for Chiara. They hadn't really developed a relationship and now the job of breaking the news to her about her daughter's plight fell on his shoulders . He fancied himself as the stoic type and would rather be risking his life on some granite wall instead of taking on matters of the heart. It was definitely his Achilles' heel.

He knew she worked at the hospital as a nurse assistant but had no idea which shift she worked . It was six o'clock in the evening on the third day of Chiara's disappearance. Jason took a deep breath, put the phone up to his ear and listened to the rings. One , two, three, four, five, and just when he thought he was off the hook, the line went live.

"Hola," said the voice on the other end.

"Hello?" Jason returned.

Immediately the other person switched from Spanish to English.

"Hello," she said.

"I'm calling for Miss Martinez," he ventured.

" This is Miss Martinez ," she said with a heavy Spanish accent.

"Hello this is Jason Bactiere; Chiara's boyfriend."

"Hello Jason! To what do I owe this honor?" she said, sensing something amiss.

Jason broke out in a fine sweat. He was a go-for-it kind of guy, so he decided not to tip toe around the topic but get right to it.

"It's not really an honor because I'm calling to see if Chiara might be there."

"Ay carumba!" she said, "are you two fighting or something?"

"Ah, no ma'am, ah Chiara disappeared three days ago and we can't seem to find her anywhere."

There was a pause while the news settled in.

"What do you mean?" she asked.

"She went for a run on Monday and never came home."

"Have you looked for her?" she asked , feeling a lump form in her throat.

"Yes, ma'am."

"Where have you looked for her?"

"I've called all her friends at work. I have gone to places we often go to climb. I have no idea where she is," Jason said, for the first time feeling vulnerable and out of control. If he just knew where she was he would go and get her.

"Have you called the police?"

"Of course, they have been here already. I filed a missing person's report the first night she didn't come home,"

"Jason, this my only child. Tell me she will still be there for me," becoming a little indignant.

"I'm sorry Miss Matinez if I could have prevented this, I would have done everything in my power to do that."

"I need to hang up now. I will be in touch with you," she said, cutting Jason off immediately. She then proceeded to stomp around her apartment, wailing and praying to God in heaven.

Jason thought about the indignation, processed it and then tried to let it go. But he was starting to feel a wave of suspicion and it was cresting on his back. Then he spent the rest of the evening on the phone recruiting as many friends as he could think of to help him look for Chiara: afterwards he drove to the Gorge to notify the climbing community.

By seven in the morning the next day, he was wide awake even though he hadn't slept much the night before. He chugged a cup of coffee with an energy bar and gazed upon an amazing sight in the lot at the front of the house. At least forty people and half as many vehicles had gathered in what he called his front yard.

A blond haired, bespectacled newspaper reporter had gotten a tip from one of the searchers and stood nearest the house in the crowd. At first, Jason was uncomfortable with the press being involved, but someone convinced him that the exposure would benefit their efforts in case someone had seen her. The reporter interviewed Jason before the search got under way.

Tommy Perkins walked over to him and for once he was very serious. He gave Jason a hug and said," We are going to find her man."

"Thanks, dude," Jason cleared his throat, "Can everyone gather around? I want to thank you all for coming out here so early. I spent the night trying to think of the most probable places Chiara might go. I think the majority of us will have to go to the Gorge, since that is such a large area and she left a note saying she was headed there."

He looked around the crowd, "Who wants to take that one on?" Jason asked. Then he picked ten people with raised hands. I'll orchestrate that group."

Jason proceeded to list five other prime spots including one group to drive to Mesquite and check out outdoor stores and other establishments for clues as to where she might be. As the group settled into their assignments , Tommy Perkins walked up to Jason.

"Hey, what if someone finds something? We need someone to man a control point, so if someone finds her car then we can all convene there," Tommy said.

"How about you do that Tommy?"

"I was thinking you would be the best one to stay here," Tommy said.

"Are you shittin' me? I'd go crazy staying here!"

"You haven't slept a wink in probably three days. You're a liability to yourself and everyone else out there."

"Jason, he's right. You don't want us to waste valuable time dragging you out of the back country," another searcher said.

The phone in Jason's house rang, abruptly ending the dialogue. Jason whirled on one foot and ran into house. He talked on the phone for several minutes while the crowd milled , mumbled and waited.

Jason walked back outside to the porch and addressed the silent waiting group of expectant faces.

"That was Chiara's mother. She's on the east bound Greyhound and she'll be here in a couple hours."

"That settles it, you have to be here when she arrives," Kyle said.

"Okay, but every group should have two cars and if you find anything you call me right away. Ia that clear?" Jason asked.

"Clear," said Tommy.

The group split up and fanned out across the region, in their rag tag convoys.

CHAPTER 10

That last dream came to Chiara again. It contained the cancer sick child from the hospital and the gray haired man. The two of them walked hand-in-hand. She rolled restlessly awake and , as always, the dream never finished before she awoke; each time at the same place. They were always walking hand-in-hand away from her; like the two of them shared a secret and did't want her to know.

Chiara's thoughts returned often during her waking hours, to the little boy who faced death with such courage. How did a child so young develop this level of bravery? Is courage an inherited quality? People definitely have different levels of this trait; but how about young children? And another thought that kept coming to her was how do children develop cancer in the first place.

The boy had constantly occupied her mind for three days she had been in this canyon prison. By now he would have been through the surgery. She said a quick prayer hoping that he had sailed through the surgery with little trauma and that the cancer was eliminated. She was constantly amazed at the resilience of young children. Thoughts of the boy brought a tear to her eye, but it was of happiness, gratefulness perhaps. In her physical pain and emotional panic, his face would come to her, reminding her of his courage. She believed that little face had given her strength to persevere. She wondered if she would ever see him or anyone, again.

The first few days of imprisonment she struggled desperately with sadness and thoughts of suicide. Jumping from the pour off in an attempt to escape, or even if the goal was suicide. But that could lead to serious injuries, pain, suffering and a slow death.

She pushed with all her might against depression; the fear and loneliness of the circumstances caused a terrible ache in her solar plexus. She decided she didn't want to die that way, shattered and broken.

She abandoned the idea of jumping. She forced herself to take several deep breaths as she let go and moved into an acceptance of her situation. On the last exhale, she committed herself to the survival of this absurd set of circumstances.

At this point in her situation, Chiara realized the slot canyon had evolved and eroded into a split of two sections. She had explored every inch of it hoping to find even the most remote chance of escape. The lower twenty five feet of the canyon was sandstone, a soft rock capped by the harder limestone, which had eroded more slowly; creating that overhanging cap.

At certain times of the day the sun made the sandstone light up into a surrealistic painting. This slot canyon was a deeply mysterious sculpture of sandstone and water, tucked away in a forlorn desert landscape and seen by few human eyes.

Chiara ran her hand over the sandy walls. They were decorated by wavy layers of multicolored striations of petrified sand. The colors ranged from yellow to orange on to brown and a bit of purple. The walls, sculpted in sensual patterns, created different moods throughout the morning, mid-day and evening. In any other scenario, the canyon would project jaw dropping beauty, unmatched by the most skilled human hands, Chiara believed. The beauty of it gifted her; the wisdom and will power to endure.

But her circumstance forced thoughts of beauty out as the practical side of her viewed the rooms, the water had taken so long to create. She designated the upper level of the sloping sculptured spaces as her bedroom because it contained a feature that would help her keep warm. As her eyes continued to scan the length of the space. she devised a way to stay warm. There was a strip of sand in the very bottom of the elongated gap.

During the day the sun would beam down into the slot warming the sand. Chiara realized she could dig a hole in the soft sand with her hands so the sun would heat the grains of sand; not only in the hole, but the also the sand piled near the hole. This only occurred at high noon. As night fell, she crawled into the warm hole and covered herself with more warm sand. This system maintained warmth for three or four hours, allowing her to sleep. As she cooled she climbed out and did her nightly dance and exercise routine to get her blood moving and spirit lifted.

During the day she took naps to compensate for the missed sleep; but also kept herself awake as much as possible to hear any human activity.

The problem of food, more accurately the lack there of, was foremost in her mind after the fourth day. She had been wearing a small fanny pack at the time of her fall. It contained a bottle of water, an energy bar and her car keys. Chiara limited herself to a quarter of the bar per day hoping rescue would come in that time. The bar was now gone.

She searched and found insects floating in the plunge pool: her stomach lurched at the thought of eating them. Several Checkered Whip-tail lizards scurried in their jerky fashion up and down the walls of the canyon capturing her attention. They or their food cache, might sustain her for some time, although it would create another challenge she felt encouraged as they scampered in their day to day existence.

Days became an elongated scratch as Chiara notched each one in the soft sandstone each evening. That led to some art work and finally a note of sorts to Jason and her mother in case they found her too late. The note was basic because her car key had worn down making it hard to hold.

A week into her odyssey Chiara lay dozing in the shaded bedroom; now in the habit of spending her days lounging naked in the sun she still chose a retreat to her bedroom for sleep because she didn't want to burn.

Craving beauty in her loneliness her eyes slipped open; the sunset retreated across the desert and dusk approached. She counted on the rich hues commonly bathed the slot canyon at that time of the day to set her body in preparation for the gathering of warmth needed for the night. But most astonishing on this evening was a sun beam angled sharply down into the canyon. The light shaft pierced into the canyon through an erosion hole up in the lip of the slot rim.

From her side view it allowed a dramatic statement of nature; especially with floating dust particles in the beam. It appeared alive, filled with energy and possibility to Chiara. Were she a more religious person, she might have wondered if God was trying to tell her something.

Death. Was it the simple end of life? Death. What is the spiritual definition? Her nurse's training defined the clinical concept. What would it feel like from the energetic perspective? Thoughts of Death drifted the young woman into a lulled state.

Death. Would she even know when her time was at hand? At the point of demise, is that the place where one's fate in the after life is decided? Heaven or hell? Is that what it is, all the pain and agony, happiness and grief, boils down to; one of two choices?

In her job as a medical professional, Chiara experienced life and death, first hand on a daily basis. She had a hard time with that notion of the complete and final END of a vibrant pulsing heart. Seeing gentle people die in the prime of their life, or before their life even had a chance to begin, or on the other end of the spectrum, the gang-bangers that gunned people down yet came through unscathed physically; would shake anyone's faith in a controlling force overseeing this world.

Chiara rose from the place in her bedroom and walked to where the sunbeam touched the wall. This time of day was often a sleep period for Chiara and that's probably why she had never seen the beam before. It was above her head so she had to step up on a ledge, two feet above the floor of the slot canyon, to touch the light.
The intense glare of the sun blinded her, so she closed her eyes and just took in the warmth rather than try to watch. "If this is the path to heaven I am ready," she thought.

Thus being transported to heaven on a light beam just now, would make a true devotee out of her. The warm beam endured ten minutes; she breathed deeply, trying to visualize riding the light up and out of the canyon.The gradual fade of warmth was replaced by a beautiful etching of the memory of calmness and peacefulness into her subconscious mind.

"Oh well," she thought.

"I guess it's hell for me!" she chuckled.

"Rather than a big expensive casket and funeral, I prefer to just rot out here in this magnificent sculpture, so maybe something else can live." She felt a lifting in her heart. Her body felt light, open and able to endure whatever must come.

CHAPTER 11

The evening remained warm and Jack shed his jacket as he walked through the lobby of the Crown Jewels Casino. He passed a counter and glanced at a newspaper that lay open revealing an article about a missing hiker. The story featured a large photo of a concerned boyfriend with the inset photo of a girl identified as the missing hiker. Other details, such as the clothing she wore and a description of her car, followed a plea for help from the community.

He read the article with interest; part of his time spent in the military was dedicated to the search and rescue of Prisoners of War. He would have helped with the search, but was too tied down with work at the casino. He disliked work overload. He had some private time this evening, so continued on through the casino.

Four security cameras tracked his movements as he headed for the front doors. He had a date with one of the blackjack dealers from the casino, but before he made it out the door a security guard approached him and whispered in his ear.

"Mr. King, Mr.Scapalini would like to see you upstairs sir," the guard said.

"What's going on now?" Jack asked , irritated.

"I don't know but he said it was very important, and that you were to see him immediately."

Jack cursed under his breath as he glanced up at the black Plexiglas domes hanging from the ceiling of the casino. He rode the elevator up and stepped off on the tenth floor and walked down the hallway to Joey's office. He slipped his jacket back on and knocked on the door. Another security guard opened the door and Jack walked in to see Joey sitting behind his desk.

"Jack we have a problem," Joey said.

Jack noticed that Joey used 'we' when there was a problem, but 'I' when there was good news.

"Yes sir?"

"I just got a call from a friend of mine who owns a strip club down town," Joey said with a frown on his face. "Vinny's down there breaking the place up and I want you to go down there and bring him home."

"No problem," Jack said knowing that his date was all but cancelled for the night.

"You didn't have any plans, did ya?"

"No sir I'll take care of the situation."

"Don't hurt him, just bring him here; and then put him to bed," Joey said, grinning.

"And here's some cash, make sure everyone's happy, " Joey handed Jack a wad of cash.

Jack nodded, and turned to leave..

"Oh Jack, take Michael here," Joey said, pointing to the other security guard in the office, "and grab someone else downstairs to help you."

Jack and the other two security people strode up to the entrance of the nightclub and bar, The Gee String. Their square shoulders and black suits made for an imposing silhouette. The bouncers controlling the door were obviously tipped off about their arrival; they simply nodded and pointed to a table by the dance floor, where a partially clad dancer struggled to get away from Vinny Scapalini.

"Come on baby, do you know who I am?" Vinny slurred, "I could make you famous, make you rich." His round head rolled around on his shoulders and his bloodshot eyes happened upon three large figures looming behind him. The crowd began to clear an area around the group as the dancer sensing trouble managed to wriggle free.

"Oh shit, Jack I can always depend on you to ruin a good time," Vinny said, spit droplets flying out of his mouth.

"Vinny, your brother wants you back at the casino," Jack said.

"My brother, it's always about my brother. It always was about my brother Joey," he stumbled back a step. "Joey, Joey, Joey. All I ever heard. And you Jack, I've had about enough of you too."

"Come on Vinny," Jack said and put his hand on Vinny's arm.

Vinny exploded into a glutinous rage. Arms and legs flailed like a goose chasing an interloper. Jack slipped an arm around Vinny's neck as the other arm reached inside his jacket to grab the nine millimeter pistol. The gun was a factor Jack didn't want added to this volatile mix. He tossed it to the floor. The sight of the gun sent the crowd squealing and stampeding for the exits. Michael found Vinny's back-up pistol strapped to his ankle and tucked it into his waistband. Then the three of them man handled Vinny out the door and towards a limo parked in front of the club. All the while Vinny screamed at them.

"When we get back to the casino, you three are fired."

"Shut up Vinny," Jack ordered.

"G.I. Joe is here," Vinny spat. "Have you ever seen a naked G.I. Joe? They don't have balls or anything else." As Vinny struggled, his pendulous belly hung out of his shirt like a full udder of a miking cow. When they arrived at the limo the two guards sat on Vinny in the backseat while Jack walked back into the club to take care of the damages.

He paid the owner a couple thousand in cash, the stripper a cool grand for her troubles, and a college kid got a couple grand to have his chipped tooth fixed. Jack looked around for the pistol he had tossed but it had disappeared.

Jack drove the group back to the casino and the three of them escorted Vinny up to a room set aside for these 'special' occasions.

In ten minutes Vinny snored like a well fed pig in the bed, while the security guard watched TV, his job was to ensure Vinny didn't choke on his vomit. Jack walked back to Joey's office but stood listening to the door before knocking. When he heard moaning coming from the other side he decided he wouldn't knock. Jack found his way to a phone in the casino and called his date for the night. No answer. She had probably given up waiting for him. Vinny was going to ruin his life, he thought.

CHAPTER 12

Consuella Martinez stepped out of the cab wearing black pants, a white shirt and a black suit jacket. Her only luggage is a small red suitcase. She is out of place walking across the yellow gravel lot, even though she strode across the lot with an air of importance. She stepped up onto the stoop and knocked sharply.

Jason opened the door and peered into a face that meant business. She was a small woman with a thin face and stress wrinkles that were framed by her black hair. He could see the resemblance to Chiara in the facial structure.. Her tight lips drew a horizontal line across her face. A barely discernible mustache sprouted from her upper lip.

"Are you Jason?" she asked.

"Yes. Miss Martinez, please come in."

"You can call me Connie."

"Okay Connie, come on in."

"Thank you. This was a hard place to find. I guess they don't believe in street numbers around here."

"It's a pretty small town. Here have a seat," Jason said pointing to the couch.

Connie perched herself on the edge of the couch. She assessed the apartment. Jason hadn't had time to clean up and the apartment was a little worse for wear. Steg jumped up on the couch and approached the visitor with caution. He voiced a tentative meow.

"That's Steg," Jason replied.

"Your cat's name is Steak?" she asked.

"No, Steg, S-t-e-g, it's short for Stegosaurus."

"Stegosaurus?"

"Connie moved her eyes sideways at the cat and Jason could see he had lost the woman in the explanation.

"You see when Chiara and I moved here he came right over to us one day; across the lot out there. He was covered with mud and that made his fur stand up on his back. He looked like the dinosaur called a Stegosaurus; they have bony spines that stick out on their spines. Chiara took pity on him, cleaned him up and he chose to stay since that bath."

"Speaking of which," she said becoming even more serious if that was possible. "Where is my daughter?"

"Connie , we are looking for her right now. I'm sorry ; if I knew where she was I'd be out there bringing her home."

For the next ten minutes he recounted the events of the last three days; what had been done and what was being done at this moment. She seemed unmoved by the efforts. And Jason understood, the fact remained her daughter was missing and no one knew where.

"It was my hope you would be able to shed some light on where she might have gone." Jason sat on the other end of the couch from the small intense woman.

"Jason do I look like I go for runs in the desert?"

"No. I just meant that you probably know things about Chiara that I don't and maybe that could help us figure out where she might be."

"Possibly," Connie paused and studied his face, wondering if he were telling the truth. A full minute of this scrutiny passed before she added, "Yes, of course Jason I will try to help in any way I can. What do you need to know?"

"For example, Chiara never talked about her father. I thought you may be able to fill in the blanks on that detail."

"The reason Chiara never talks about her father is because he died when she was one year old."

"Go on," Jason said to encourage the woman.

"You see Jason, when I was sixteen and living in Spain, I met a man; a man that was much older than I. He was a very powerful man. When he entered a room, he had the kind of presence and charm that turns heads. I was immediately attracted to him. One thing led to another and suddenly, the inevitable. I became pregnant. I knew my parents would disown me should they find out. So my lover gave me enough money to get to the United States."

Jason sat stroking Steg on his lap as the story unfolded.

"We were very poor but made it to Los Angeles. I was fluent in Spanish so I found jobs where I could translate after I learned enough English. It was a difficult life."

"I had to work two jobs and that forced Chiara to grow up fast and on her own for the most part. She left home as soon as she could to find her way to a life in the wilderness. She is a very self sufficient young woman, as you well know."

"What was her father's name?" Jason asked.

"He was an American by birth, his name was Ernesto, but I often called him Papa. I don't discuss it often, because in my society it is associated with a lot of shame. But there is one thing that Chiara doesn't know, and I would never have revealed to anyone if this hadn't come up."

Jason leaned in; sensing a key piece of information may be forthcoming.

"I've always told Chiara that her father died in a car accident because I didn't want her to be burdened with this." Connie paused to gather her composure. " The truth is Ernesto committed suicide a year after Chiara was born."

The breath swished out of Jason, as if stomach punched. All the events of the past months began to gather on the horizon like a desert thunderstorm.

"When you called , suicide was the first thing I worried about; that this legacy of mental illness had resurfaced."

"Wow, so her father had mental illness also." Jason was stunned. Suddenly, Chiara's mood swings over the last few months seemed a lot more serious.

"How has she been acting?" Connie asked .

"She's had some episodes of sadness. Sometimes she just sits around the house; she can't seem to get the motivation to do any of the thing's we like doing."

Connie's secret fears realized; the anguish showed on her face.

"But then she'll come out of it and things will be fine;
like the good old times," Jason said, trying to reassure her.

"That's why I took time off and got on the first bus here."

There was a pause in the conversation as both of them got lost in their own thoughts. Jason couldn't imagine Chiara committing suicide; he just didn't think she had it in her, but there were so many loose ends.

Where was her car? People did leave suicide notes; but Chiara's didn't read morose. She wasn't particularly up beat either, but that was to be expected with the night she had at work. Jason walked to the table and picked up the note and handed it to Connie.

"Is there any chance she wants to leave you; any chance there is another man?" Connie asked, starring straight into Jason eyes. She wasn't a woman who minced words. And as she watched him a glossier sheen developed over his eyes. He shook his head and walked out to the stoop and squatted down, so his eyes could dry.

A few minutes later Connie came outside, put her hand on Jason's shoulder.

Jason shook his head again, "Well I don't feel there was, but I would probably be the last to know that information."

So I have one more difficult question for you, Connie said , "Are you seeing anyone else?"

He was shocked and almost told her it wasn't any of her business, but he decided to just inhale and then let out a long sigh," Oh course not," Jason said.

Silence followed the uncomfortable interchange until thankfully, the phone rang. "Jason this is Kyle." Jason's heart began pounding in his chest," We've been all over Zion from one end to the other , "Kyle hesitated for a moment." We didn't see one thing that might be a lead." Jason felt his shoulders drop.

"What are you goin' to do now?" Jason asked.

"It getting kind of late," Kyle said, "I think we might call it a day, unless you can think of some place else for us."

"If you would just go to the ranger station and leave a description of her and the car, I'd appreciate it," Jason said.

"Sure buddy," Kyle said.

"Thanks, I'll keep in touch."

Jason hung up the phone and tried to smooth the frown off his face, five more calls came in with the same news. No one had found even the slightest clue to Chiara's whereabouts.

Connie's frame of mind slipped a notch lower with each call.

After the last call Jason offered to take her back to Mesquite so she could get a hotel room. He dropped her off and promised to call if he heard anything.

CHAPTER 13

A week after their trip to St. George to see Rake Rains, Vinny and Jack sat in Joey's office at the Crown Jewels Casino. The trip had been a watershed event of sorts for the three. Joey held Jack in much higher esteem for the way he handled the entire situation with Rake. Jack had even more disdain for Vinny, cowering in fear inside the Hummer, while Jack got all the work done.

Joey was pleased about his decision to move Jack up in the organization; the guy truly had balls that would not quit. Joey was pleased he had moved Jack into head of security. Vinny would be pissed when he found out but he knew he could handle that.

His brother was like a loose cannon; stirring things up all the time. Vinny was worse after the trip out to the Rains ranch. He hated Jack even more since he had been made to look like a fool. Since that trip he had been drunk most of the time.

"I need you two to go back out and visit the old man," Joey said, "See if he is any closer to accepting the offer."

The tension in the room notched higher; Joey hoped Jack's ability to handle situations would rub off on Vinny.

"I can't make this trip," Joey said as he watched the scowl form on Vinny's face. "I have to meet with the gaming commissioner. But I don't want to lose the momentum of the deal."

"Yes sir," Jack said.

"I don't have a gun, jerk wad lost mine when he assaulted me in the bar last night," Vinny complained as he pointed toward Jack.

Joey reached into his jacket and pulled out his own Glock pistol and handed it to Vinny.

"Here just get this back to me when you return, and one more thing Vinny; Jack's in charge on this one, follow his lead."

"You know if our father was still around, he would put you in your place," Vinny blurted out.

"Well he's not around; do I make myself clear?"
Joey asked. "If I'm ruining your party out here, Joey, I'll be glad to go back to AC and do my own thing," Vinny said.

"Go ahead," Joey said, "and you'll be dead in two weeks."

The verbal battle between the two continued most of the way back to Rake Rains place and the vehemence between Jack and Vinny hung heavy in the air. Vinny was especially pissed because he was blood to his fathers inheritance, and he didn't like taking a submissive role to this hired gun. Vinny's mind whirred with ideas for how to re-establish himself. Jack was aware he was on the fast track in the organization so he chose to ignore Vinny who seethed constantly with anger.

"Jack you know I'm not stupid in the ways of this lifestyle; things happen, accidents happen. You might just disappear one day," Vinny growled.

"Well, I tell you what Vinny, when we get to Rake's place you can play with his dogs while I close this deal," Jack said laughing.

"What the fuck are we doing this stupid shit for anyway? Are we boy scouts ?"
Vinny complained.

"Why don't we just run the casino?"

"It's about control," Jack said, realizing that comment would most likely pass right over Vinny's head. "If your brother can control the water around here; he can control everything. That's why he wants to buy Bruja Canyon."

"Brouha ha! I wish I could have a Brewski right now!" he shouted out.

Vinny glared at Jack. "Why would anybody name this place Brouha, unless they planned to open a bar?"

"Bruja; is Spanish for witch," Jack replied pronouncing the word correctly.

"I've known a few of those," Vinny said. Then returned to his quiet angry place and glared for the rest of the ride.

Jack thought Vinny might take revenge on him but Jack was used to being in the company of dangerous men. Vinny was all talk and threats and took action only if he were heavily favored to win. Jack also knew the loud, angry types were less of a threat then the quiet, sneaky ones.

Jack swung the Hummer into the drive of Rake's property and saw a dust cloud fading to the east.

He stopped the Hummer, got out and yelled a greeting at the house, but no sound returned. He surmised Rake was likely in the vehicle they saw heading east. A mile east of the house they found Rake working on a fence line near the mouth of Bruja Canyon.

The canyon opening, although narrow was nonetheless imposing. The rock formation locale was so impressive that Jack almost missed the old yellow Subaru parked under the tree on the opposite side of the wash from where they found Rake. He made a mental note of the car's position and stepped out of the vehicle to greet Rake.

"Hello Mr. Rains," Jack said, striding out from the Hummer. Low growls greeted him. The dogs continued to lay on the flat bed of the truck.

"Down," Rake scolded and they stifled their complaints. "You boys again?"

"Hello sir," Jack said smiling. He extended his hand in greeting, but Rake failed to reciprocate.

Vinny, tired of Jack getting all the attention, scurried out of the vehicle. He had concluded the dogs were all bluff. Simultaneously the muscled dogs barked and jumped up, as if getting a read on Vinny. The canine heads lowered as snarls vibrated the ridgeback hair stiff with warning. Coarse whiskers quivered as drawn back lips grimaced a guttural sound of hostility. One inch canines shimmered and slimed in the desert light. Four slitted eyes burned fire.

Vinny stepped forward. The dogs leapt for him off the back of the flatbed. He lurched into the now seething animals. Vinny had his hand on the Glock his brother had given him. The rest happened so fast that even Jack was surprised. But self preservation took over for the two dogs and all three men and then all hell broke loose. That's when the nightmare started.

Jack's face flushed livid. He hated losing control of a situation. Control was what he did best; in fact control was what he breathed.

"You asshole," Jack screamed , as he sped down the highway.

"Why is every thing my fault, you didn't have a handle on things, I had to take over," Vinny whined, " and where were you when I needed help?"

"Everything was fine until you had to take your fat ass out of the Hummer," Jack chided.

"Well that place is haunted," Vinny whined.

"Now it is."

"Are you going to take me to a hospital?"

"Shut up I need time to think."

"But those dogs tore my hand up."

Jack tossed a bottle of Vicodin to Vinny," Take a couple of those."

Jack's mind raced. He forced himself to get a grip, if the cops stopped them it would be all over. He released some of the pressure on the accelerator and the Hummer sagged back toward the speed limit. He couldn't believe his luck. One day a rising star in this new enterprise, the next day he was headed for disaster. He would really have to watch his step now.

Jack wore a tank top covered with dirt and torn on the bottom. His muscular shoulders and arms were covered with dust streaked by sweat rivulets. A tattoo of three human footprints, green in color, graced his shoulder. It was the mark of the elite; Special Forces.

Vinny was covered with lacerations and blood, a special treat from Mack and Sally.

The headlights reached into the silent falling night. The air whistled in through the open window; mostly drowning out Vinny's whimper. Jack noticed lights on in Joey's office on the tenth floor as he pulled into the garage. They took the service elevator; it was empty at this time of night. Jack knew his survival at this point depended on deflecting the heat Vinny had created with his impulsive choices.

As the two of them exited the Hummer, he stepped in close to Vinny, grabbed him under his good arm, then half carried half dragged the now hysterical hulk toward Joey's office door. Vinny's arms were covered with blood and dog bites. One hour later an aging doctor who was on the 'staff' of the casino walked in with a medical bag. The lights in Joey's office were on until morning.

Joey kept a condo in Acapulco, Mexico for family vacationing and as incentives to use for select business people. If an important deal was in the works and the client couldn't decide, they were offered a free vacation in Acapulco. Two days later, Vinny was on a plane to Mexico for a vacation from the rigors of his security job.

CHAPTER 14

Paperwork sprawled out across his desk as Detective Jones leaned back in his chair with fingers interlaced behind his head. He contemplated the evidence; skimpy as it was. Endless places flashed through his mind to hide bodies in this area; and he didn't even have that much knowledge of the backcountry. The rock climbing boyfriend could accomplish hiding a body without raising a sweat, he thought. But what might be the motivation to kill his girl friend?

Jones reviewed the day of interviews in Littlefield, and surrounding environs. Nothing jumped out at him, Jason, the psycho lady, the climbers; they all seemed relatively harmless.

What had he missed? Something unsettling about the elderly woman that spent her days screaming at invisible demons bothered him. The old lady was certainly interesting but in her own parallel universe. It was difficult to separate reality from fantasy.

What had she been mumbling about that day? Some off the wall comment about Germany, and that repeated comment about a dead dog. And what was that last item; 'a big black bag'. Did she see something?

Had the rock climbing gang seen someone in the car with Chiara or whoever was driving, when the car pulled into the parking area at the Gorge? Did that someone make her leave when he or she saw the crowd? Was that even Chiara's car? He had a strong feeling that this was one of those cases that would end up in the cold case file.

He made a to-do list and had a feeling he would be heading back to Littlefield soon. He picked up the phone and dialed a number in his phone book. Two rings and the party on the other end picked up.

"Dr. Waxley, " the woman's voice stated.

Dr. Lila Waxley ran the Arizona State Hospital for the mentally ill, and RJ had used her expertise in past cases.

"Dr. Waxley, Detective Jones here, Arizona State Police.

"Hello, Detective," Dr. Waxley replied in her clinical monotone way.

"How's it going doctor?"

"Detective, I'm a doctor of the mentally insane; every day's a new challenge."

"I hear ya there," RJ said.

"How can I help you Detective?" Dr, Waxley asked, already tiring of the small talk.

"I'm working on a case up in Littlefield, and there is a potential witness who suffers from schizophrenia. I'm trying to make sense of what she told me. How much of her words might be delusional and how much could be reality?"

"It's different with every patient; it could be some, all or none."

"Is there any way to determine what's true or false?"

"Maybe, what is her demeanor?"

"She seems very angry."

"You'll probably have to gain her trust, so she's not so threatened; that may or may not be possible."

RJ thanked the doctor and hung up the phone. Maybe another trip to Littlefield would be just what the doctor ordered, he thought.

The following morning RJ said goodbye to his wife, fired up the Crown Vic and pointed it towards the northwest. Covering this huge territory was the worse part of his job for him but the freedom of working autonomously was very attractive. Three hours later he rolled into Littlefield and headed directly for the elderly woman in the triangle.

RJ approached the woman with the biggest smile he could honestly muster. The woman's gray messy hair stuck out at odd angles and dark bags hung down under her mistrusting eyes.

He stepped out of his car and was greeted with a hard stare.

"Hello ma'am,? RJ said. "Ma'am, I could really use your help since I know, you know everything that happens in this town. You are such a good observer." RJ continued, "What's your name?"

Still she didn't speak. RJ felt it was promising that at least she wasn't screaming at him maybe he was gaining her confidence.

"My name is RJ, and I think we could be a good team," he said.

"So are we a team; OK? What's your name?"

"Eva Braun, my name is Eva Braun. Okay, arrest me if you have to."

"No, that won't be necessary," RJ said suddenly losing faith in this attempt to gain a grain of valuable information. He remembered what Dr. Waxley had said; it seemed that this old woman was beyond any helpful level of reality. He tried one more time.

"You look really well, Eva. I don't want you to worry about anything that happened in the past, don't worry about Germany or anything else. Just focus on the right now, on this week,"RJ said.

"Can you tell me what happened last Monday? That was six days ago."
RJ said, trying to be patient.

"I told you he was hiding something in that big bag," she said, her eyes darting from side to side. She still hadn't made eye contact with RJ.

Yeah RJ thought. That's the topic he wanted to revisit, but how reliable would it be?
Oh well it wouldn't hurt to hear what she might say, as long as he took it with a grain of salt.

"Was he hiding something in that big bag?" RJ repeated what she had just said,to jog her memory.

"Yeah there was something in that bag," she said pointing to Jason's house. RJ turned and shaded his eye's with his hand, and gazed upon the house and on the space around the house. He knew anything she said was not admissible in court; a defense attorney would take it all apart. He came to the conclusion he would have to find something else. Looking in that house across the way was probably his best bet. RJ thanked Mrs. Braun, or whoever she was, then swung his vehicle across the road onto the lot where Jason lived.

Jason saw RJ pull into the triangle and immediately had a sinking feeling. It was a major disappointment regarding the location of Chiara If the detective had found any clue about her whereabouts, he would have come to the house first. Jason walked out to greet him.

"Hello detective," Jason said," have you heard anything?"

"I was going to ask you the same thing," the detective responded. "I heard you sent search parties out."

"I can't just sit here and twiddle my thumbs."

"I wish you would run these things by me before you do them. You could be wiping out crucial evidence; that action could be misconstrued as obstruction of an investigation. Besides I heard you were sitting here while everyone else was out searching," RJ said trying to evoke some emotion.

Jason sensed a change in the detectives demeanor. He suddenly felt uncomfortable and pushed into the spotlight but tried to keep his composure.

"We decided it would be best for me to stay here and orchestrate all the different angles of the search," Jason said. "Trust me it wasn't easy for me to stay here, but Chiara's mother rolled onto town and I wanted to update her on the facts so far."

"Excellent," RJ said," I'll need to talk to her also."

"She will be here in a couple hours."

"Good," RJ said stretching the word out and nodding his head. "Say Jason, do you have a big black duffle bag?"

"Yeah, I do," he said pausing momentarily. "I totally forgot, I put it in the back of my truck, I was going to do my laundry that morning; but with all the excitement, I forgot about it."

Jason walked over to the back of his pickup and reached for the back door on his topper. As it squeaked open the reality of RJ's eyes watching his every move evoked the feeling that every word or inflection of his voice was being monitored. The realization he was now considered a suspect in the disappearance of Chiara Martinez made a lump form in his throat.

"How did you know about the black bag?" Jason asked looking over at the elderly woman.

"I've been doing this for twenty years, Jason. I have my ways."

"Yeah, all of a sudden you have eyes and ears everywhere."

"Are you hiding something?"

"Of course not," Jason said indignant at the question.

The boxing gloves were definitely off now and Jason's mindset cooled.

"Can I look in this bag?"

"Of course as I said I have nothing to hide. If dirty laundry is your thing, go for it."

RJ opened the bag and realized this was not the place for the inspection of possible evidence.

"I'm going to take this to the police station down the street so I don't mess your clothes up here in the dust."

"That's almost all of my clothes; when am I going to get them back?"

"Maybe right away; but I have to tell you that I may have to impound them as evidence."

"What?" Jason blurted out.

RJ lifted the heavy bag into the trunk of his car. Next, he drove directly to the Littlefeild chief of police and explained his purpose and his needs. The chief led him to a holding cell where he could inspect the contents of the black bag in an orderly manner.

RJ slipped on a pair of latex gloves and took the items out the bag piece by piece. He bagged certain items that he thought might hold some significance.

Then he arrived at the bright yellow tee shirt. As he opened the garmet he knegarmentw the feel of it just wasn't right; a slight adhesion of the fabric impeded the opening of the shirt.
Before getting the shirt fully open RJ could see the shirt was covered with blood.

He bagged the shirt and turned to the chief.

"I'm going to need a runner to take this stuff down to the lab in Phoenix," RJ said.

"I'll make it happen," the chief said.

"But first, I'm going to need to get some more items from the house, why don't you send an officer back to house with me."

"Marshall, run back to the house with the detective."

"Yes sir," Marshall said, then followed RJ back to his car.

Two hours after leaving Jason to bathe in his own sweat, RJ pulled back into the front lot at the house. RJ and the patrolman walked into the house and found Jason pacing back and forth. Conseulo Martinez sat on the edge of the couch.

"Hello," RJ said to the woman. "I'm Detective Jones from the Arizona State Police and I'm leading the investigation into Chiara's disappearance."

"Hello, sir" Connie said wrinkles furrowing her forehead.

"Can I ask you a few questions?" RJ asked.

RJ asked the standard questions about family, possible health conditions, mental health issues from her past that might just be related to this case. And of course her relationship with Jason. Jason sat on the coffee table listening to the questions and replies. He watched as RJ jotted down notes. Patrolman Marshall stood by the door with his arms across his chest.

After the interview RJ turned to Jason and said, "Jason I need to look through your house again."

"I need you to give me an explanation first," Jason said rather gruffly near the end of his patience. Marshall perked up sensing an aggressive tone.

"What kind of an explanation do you need?" RJ responded.

"Why have you gotten so interested in this house? She's obviously not here!" Jason said.

"We've got a little problem Jason," RJ responded.

"No you've got a big problem. My girlfriend," Jason said forcefully, gesturing toward Connie," her daughter is missing and you arc doing nothing to find her."

"That's not true. We're chasing down leads," RJ said.

"Am I a suspect?" Jason asked.

"At this time I'm not in a position to rule on who is a suspect," RJ answered.

"Now back to the other problem," RJ said," we found a bloody tee shirt in your laundry bag."

Normally stern-faced Connie tensed and her eyes grew wide as her head swung to look back at Jason. Her mouth dropped open as she focused, now speechless, on the man next to her. Facial muscles flexed her jaw.

"Well," Jason said with an uncomfortable pause. He had been caught by surprise by the presence of a bloody tee shirt.

"Chiara occasionally has a bloody nose. That's how that shirt got bloody! I had forgotten about about that." Jason said somewhat defensively. His face flushed crimson during the interchange. Everyone in the room took notice.

"So you are telling me that the blood on that tee shirt is Chiara's?" RJ said "Yes, it came out of her nose, that would make it her blood,"

Jason said turning to Connie. "she must have had nose bleeds when she was young. She has a lot of them now."

"Not that I recall," Connie said.

"Well this is a dry climate," Jason said.

"I'm going to need a source of DNA for Chiara, do you have a hair brush or anything?" RJ asked.

"In the bathroom," Jason said, motioning with his head.

"Marshall," RJ said turning to the officer. The uniformed cop walked into the bathroom and returned with a hairbrush in a zip lock bag.

"Is that it?" RJ asked Jason.

"Yep."

"It will also be helpful for us to obtain samples from both of you, for comparison purposes."

RJ took swabbed saliva from Jason and Connie. Then he walked around the house one more time stopping to look at photos of Chiara and Jason during happier times in the wilderness areas around the American West.

"The officers in Littlefeild are going to keep tabs on you over the next few days," RJ said looking directly at Jason. "Don't take any long trips."

Jason watched him; silently grinding his teeth.

RJ and Marshall left the house and returned to the station. Within the hour Marshall was on the road to Phoenix.

Jason sighed and dropped to the couch; bouncing slightly as he hit. Connie stood and turned to face Jason with a look of distress.

"If you did anything to my only child," she said with a sneer that only a mother can make when she thinks her child has been hurt, "I will make sure you rot in hell. She spun and stomped out the door. She walked directly to her rental car, climbed in and drove away.

Jason stared blankly at the wall. Steg jumped up onto the couch and stared silently at the man who supplied his meals on ocassion.

"Why is everyone looking at me like I'm a murderer?" he said to the cat. "Five days ago Chiara was here giggling and laughing. Three days from now I may be in prison. How do I defend myself?" The cat responded with a squeaky meow to the rhetorical question.

CHAPTER 15

Chiara walked to her calendar in the bedroom of the slot canyon; eight scratches on the wall. She had also managed to etch her name into the soft sand stone wall. If she died before they found her car and contacted Jason, they would be able to identify her body, even it it was years later. Lack of food began to take it's toll; she couldn't move around without serious dizziness. But then she remembered stories of people lasting forty days on a huger strike with no food. However, when she looked at her face in the pool of water she saw cheekbones pushing into the skin under her eyes. Each day the twin orbs sunk further back into her skull. The effect left unoccupied hollow spaces in where her cheeks used to reside.

Chiara thought, "This may be my final resting place." Her mind filled with frustration and confusion.

"Why can't they find my car parked right down at the mouth of this canyon?" she whispered to the wind that howled. Each day up and down the canyon it whirled as air temperatures fluctuated between hot afternoon and cool evening shifted day into night.

The next morning started her ninth day of captivity. Hearing an unusual noise beyond the wind moan, she turned to investigate. She located and followed a pathetic whine and then whimpering sound.

The near human voice made the hair on the back of her neck stand and her scalp tingle. It came a third time and she froze to listen more closely. As the whimper ended, she turned her head slowly to get a better angle on the sound or maybe catch a glimpse of something.

The noises came again, a bit more determined than before. The resonance originated above her. The emaciated woman looked up at the pour off from which she had initially fallen. A matted furry face looked down upon her. Her breath startled, not sure of what she saw.

Was she actually seeing, or was it hallucinations? Upon closer inspection she felt sure the face belonged to a real dog. It's tongue hung out to one side as it panted in short nervous increments. Silent now; it stared at her.

Shock and fear waved through her at the sight of this vision; even though the animal seemed as stunned by the turn of events as she.

Chiara was now unsure how to proceed. She didn't want to miss this opportunity for company of some kind, but allowing a wild animal in the canyon with her could become a fight for her life.

Was it a wild animal? As breath expelled from her, she took a longer look, this time directly into eyes of the animal. No, it was a dog, not a coyote or fox. That meant it must have an owner nearby. But something wasn't right with this animal.

It's face seemed to be covered with a dark goo and it appeared weak. The dog stood near the edge of the pour off. In her shock, Chiara didn't move as she stared at the now wobbling dog.

At that first sign of an injury, Chiara's nursing instinct kicked in and cancelled out the fear factor. At that precise moment, the animal collapsed into a fall from the lip of the pour off to drop exactly into the plunge pool just as Chiara had done.

Her skin crawled with fear and at the same moment, she readied her self for action; immediately she felt another kind of shock and became locked in place for a second time. That sort of frozen place where five seconds seems like five minutes. Memories of personal terror rushed through her to momentarily causing her to freeze in place. The dog hit the water, sinking completely under and then floated limply to the top of the water in the pool. The sudden emergency moved Chiara into the life saving mode as she jumped into action.

She half waded, half jumped into the pool and drug the dog out before remembering she had no training for lifesaving measures on an animal. But she continued to look closely at the unconscious dog; to asses the damage. She recoiled in horror as the dog's head came into focus. It did have blood on the face and it appeared to be seeping from a hole below it's eye that entered on top of it's nose and exited out the underside of it's neck; in the loose folds of skin.

Working in a modern day emergency department, she had seen her share of gunshot wounds. This was definitely a through and through wound; typical of gunshot wounds. She was sure that this animal would die in a matter of hours, or wake up in a snarling rage as a result of the pain. Still her lifesaving mind kicked in and she dragged the dog up onto the sand. Chiara left the dog stretched out on the sand knowing that there was nothing she could do for this animal. She decided to let fate run it's course.

After long moments of no movement, she walked over to a piece of driftwood that had wedged into a crack. After collecting herself, she struggled it free, taking frequent rests. In the end she had a dried, water polished piece of wood roughly the size of a baseball bat.

If the second of the two possible options for this animal came to pass, she would need a weapon to defend herself.

Chiara sat and watched the dog and counted the slow steady respirations. The breaths continued through the day, but the animal never moved. She was afraid to sleep, but as night fell she walked back down to the bottom pour off, away from the prostrate dog. If she couldn't fight the animal off, she would jump. Eventually she lost the battle against sleep and dozed off, leaning over her club.

She jerked awake with the first light and was immediately tense. Afraid to turnaround she sensed another presence. When she finally summoned the courage to look, she couldn't believe the image that was before her.

A tan colored dog, broad in the shoulders but slim in the waist, sat on the upper rock ledge with it's head cocked to one side and it's tail gently sweeping from side to side.

Chiara managed to take a breath and begin to relax as the amazement wore off. A dog, that she had given up for dead, twelve hours before, sat wagging it's tail as if to gently greet her.

She had always been amazed at the resiliency of animals, but these past hours ventured almost beyond belief. After a time she reached out with a tentative hand and the dog, now almost revived, came forward to lick her hand, it's tail still wagging, but now more vigorously.

"It's okay!" she whispered. "It's okay. What happened to you? How did you get here?" Chiara said.

She couldn't believe this incredible twist of fate; as if an omen of hope had dropped out of the sky.

"You must have either smelled the water or smelled me and found your way here!" She scratched the dog's belly and took the opportunity to examine it further.

She had many other scrapes and cuts, but the gunshot wound was the worse. The wound was a large caliber and as the dog breathed it caused a high pitched squeal. A flap of skin lifted off it's chin with every exhalation but the dog didn't seem to mind, perhaps distracted by it's new found friend.

Jack pushed himself back on the couch and took three deep breaths and held each one before releasing them slowly. He watched the people on the screen and waited for the voices and words to reach his ears and catch up with the images on the fifty-two inch screen television. It was his last gift from Joey. His boss could be a generous man when he felt the need to reward his employees. The scene in Jack's apartment was his version of resting. He liked the TV and usually watching it would unwind him. Tonight it was not working.

Doubts shimmered through his mind that maybe he had missed an important detail. The events of the last couple days could land him in prison for the rest of his life. A need for control rose like bile in the back of his throat; it carved at his mind.

The disappearance of the nurse who lived up the road from Mesquite flashed across the screen. Photos of the early twenties woman and her car popped up on the screen again during a news piece.

Jack's conscious awareness flooded with deep thoughts of what he should do now. Then, he remembered an old yellow Subaru parked under a tree by the entrance of Bruja canyon. That spark of detail had gotten buried in the scattered excitement of that day; the day Jack lost control of a critical situation.

Continued news bulletins regarding the young woman sparked Jack's mind. Of course! The girl must have gotten hurt in the back country. Soon, someone would see that car and figure things out, and then the search would be on. Jack couldn't allow crowds of searchers into that area; not to mention search dogs.

Immediately he went directly to the casino and found Joey eating dinner in the VIP section of the restaurant.

"Jack, please join me," Joey said gesturing to the empty chair across from him, "this veal is exquisite. Want some?"

"No thank you."

"Well at least have a little wine with me," Joey said. The waiter poured another glass. Jack sat down.

"I need to speak with you.... privately," Jack said looking around at the hovering staff.

Joey waved his hand casually palm down and the wait staff slipped out of the room.

"Jack you look distressed. What's the matter?'

"We have a potentially huge problem," Jack responded.

"What's up?"

Jack described what he had seen on the news and his suspicions. The two of them sketched out a plan and Jack jumped into action.

Control kissed his cheek as he drove to the local moving truck rental shop to procure a large truck with a box and a loading ramp. Gathering the rest of the tools he needed, Jack swung the truck onto the highway and headed north. He was very happy to be working totally alone. He was the one person he knew he could depend on. More than anything his relief to be rid of Vinny for a while elevated his mood profusely. By two o'clock in the the morning, Jack sat in the cab of the rental truck about two miles from the mouth of Bruja canyon.

He fitted the night vision goggles on and made the necessary adjustments, then hiked up to the mouth of Bruja working his way slowly in case anyone happened to be out in the thick black night.. When he reached the right place he settled down to observe the area for any activity. A fox ran up the expansive creek bed in search of food, but nothing resembling humans moved. The car glowed green in the goggles and Jack eased himself down from his perch and over to it. It was locked. He slipped a spring loaded center punch out of his pocket and with a small thud the window dissolved into fragments. He reached in to unlock the door and climbed in.

Once inside he jammed a large screwdriver into the ignition and cranked the engine. After five seconds, the engine turned over. Next he leaned his powerful arms into the steering wheel twisting until the lock in the steering column snapped. Slowly he eased the yellow Subaru back down the gravel road using his night vision goggles so he wouldn't have to turn on the headlights.

He drove the two miles back to the truck, up the ramp and into the back of the truck. After securing the little car inside, he pulled up the ramps, rolled the door down and padlocked it. Dawn cracked open the eastern horizon just as Jack pulled into the casino garage. He unloaded the car, covered it with a tarp in the garage and was walking out as Joey approached. He was just coming to work and Jack gave him the play by play.

"It's very important that nobody knows about this," Joey said, "Now that the only obstacle is out of the picture, I'm having my attorney's work on acquiring the land, in a couple years all the evidence will be under water."

"Are you sure Vinny won't talk," Jack said, "When he gets drunk he tends to lose control of his tongue.

"Vinny is family Jack. I'll take care of him," Joey replied.

"If he screws up we could all be in prison."

"Jack, don't tell me how to run this place. I know the price of Vinny screwing up; I've had to deal with it my entire life."

Jack wished Joey would take care of it all; once and for all. The opportunity was never better with Vinny in Mexico. An accident could be easily arranged in that still relatively wild country. But he knew that family was untouchable to the Scapalini's. Jack left Joey's office to go home and collapse into bed.

Chiara spent the day getting to know her new roommate. The initial moments of apprehension faded quickly as the friendship formed. The beginning of it all happened when she chose to wrap her shirt around the dog's injured head to hold the flap secure. The scent of her filled the dog with tenderness.

Obviously a mix of breeds, it had short tan hair covering it's sleek body. The most unusual aspect of the animal was the near black hair along it's spine seemed to be growing in the wrong direction. This fact caused it to stand vertically and when she stroked it with the palm of her hand, it gave her a tickling sensation. A smile softened her face and lent hope to her soul.

She had cleaned the wounds tentatively at first; worried she might hurt the dog and
cause it to react in pain. It was a gentle surprise when the dog leaned into her massage to enjoy the attention and nurturing. Chiara relaxed and the tentative bond between animal and human grew.

If the owner of this dog would come to reclaim it, her day would be perfect.

"So, what do I call you?" Chiara asked the animal. The tail wagged in response.

"if we're going to spend time together, I can't just be yelling 'hey you' to get your attention.

The dog lay down to rest it's head on the out stretched paws. Brown eyes watched every move she made. A master of non-verbal communication, the female ridgeback cross lifted her head when Chiara moved her lips slightly into a small smile.

"Well. how about 'Girl'?" she asked, then laughed at the Tarzan-like simplicity of the name; next she said, "Me Woman, you Girl?" followed by another giggle. In the middle of the joke the dog barked which scared Chiara into silence. She had never been a dog owner but not because she didn't like dogs, instead her current transient lifestyle was not conducive to it. It soon became evident to Chiara that the animal was enjoying the joke too.

"Okay you don't like that, maybe something a little more dignified?"

Chiara thought back to different books she had read. And then it came to her.

"How about 'Isa' Let's see Isa, what does that mean? Hmm oh yeah I looked that up when I was in high school. It was one of my favorite names, and it is the female name for iron, well you definitely have that covered. And considering what you've been through that's very appropriate. Now can we make a deal?" Isa just laid there watching Chiara.

"Okay it's settled then; Isa. "I'm Chiara, friends forever?,," and she put her hand out to shake at which point Isa extended her paw. The gesture cemented the team.

The rest of the day flowed as every other day had, except Chiara now had something with which to share the boredom. This quirky event became a catalyst for her survival.

She thought about the advantages of a dog. A pair of canine ears to listen for sounds, day or night, a loud dog bark to summon help, another warm body during the cold nights and of course a shoulder to cry on at the lowest of points. The treasure of this gift that literally fell from the sky, overwhelmed her. Tears of joy slipped silently down her gaunt cheeks and her stomach growled with emptiness.

That sound and feeling cancelled out the negative thoughts of how a dog trapped here with her who was just as hungry. The pain of hunger could wreak havoc on both of them. She couldn't bear to think her new friend might be forced to turn on her. She pushed the thought out of her mind, but in the shadows of her soul, she knew she would jump if Isa became a danger. After all maybe Isa could catch one of those lizards that scrambled around the canyon. The taste of sweet white lizard meat flitted through her mind.

CHAPTER 16

RJ had spent the night in a motel in Mesquite. Northwestern Arizona was seriously short on quality accommodations. The case had started to produce some positive leads. Jason's story was convincing but there were too many red flags. RJ went through the possibilities again to try and make one of them fit. Suicide was a probability due to the young woman's state of mind reported by both Jason and Connie, but the note that she left was not a suicide note.

On the other hand the note she left for Jason was not very passionate; maybe infidelity was the motive? Of course, there were strong odds that she was kidnapped, but not for money; between them they barely had enough to pay their bills.

There was the option of a sexual assault that led to murder, if intentional; manslaughter if by accident. It was not that uncommon for that kind of violent end in this desert country. However it continued to be a big unknown regarding Chiara. Only a body could prove that at this point. RJ thought the vehicle seen at the Gorge was the best possible lead. He wanted to know, if she had someone else controlling her moves on the day of her disappearance. Where is the car, finding that would answer a lot of questions.

RJ placed a call to the State Police Crime Lab in Phoenix, Arizona. The lab was among the most advanced in the country, especially on DNA analysis. After several transfers RJ ended up with the evidence technician contacted by Marshall. The blood on the tee shirt was most likely that of Chiara Martinez based on the sample obtained from her hairbrush. The technician said it would take a week or more to get a conclusive match admissible in court. This clue was mildly helpful, but Jason had already reported the blood as coming from Chiara's nosebleed.

RJ knew he would have to get the crime lab guys in that house to see if there was any microscopic evidence lingering that he and the patrolman failed to find. Transferred to the mobile crime lab team coordinator RJ was informed they had been very busy and the mobile team would be tied up for a few days. The money hadn't caught up with the science of crime scene investigation, and the techs were few in numbers. The coordinator suggested he should secure the premises in the interim.

RJ called his office and another detective picked up the line.

"Hey RJ where have you been?" the detective asked.

"This case is starting to produce leads and I need to stay out here in country."

"There was another disappearance in that area."

"Talk to me,"RJ said

"Some guy is missing less than fifty miles north of your case, but it's out of our jurisdiction."

"Where?"

"Just across the line in Utah. Northwest of St. George."

"Give me the details."

"Hang on a second," the detective said and reached for a sheet of information on RJ's desk, "Sixty six year old white male, lives alone, everything in his house is untouched, cars are there, but he hasn't been seen for about a week. A friend stopped by to check on him, said the horses hadn't been fed."

"Any sign of my Yellow Subaru?" RJ asked.

"That would be a negative. I just thought you'd want to know, this case is pretty close to the area of your case."

"Thanks for the information, hey transfer me in to the captain."

RJ spoke with the division captain, then hung up and called the chief in Littlefeild. He gave him instructions to seal off Jason's house until the crime scene team could get up there. Jason would have to find other accommodations.

An hour later he was driving north across the state line to check out this other disappearance.

The dust settled thick on RJ's white cruiser. He had followed a Utah State Patrol vehicle down a dirt road to a beat up shanty up against a one hundred foot cliff. RJ slid out of the driver's seat and looked around. This was the perfect defensive position he thought; no one could sneak up on this house. The highway patrolman led the way as they walked into the house.

"Has the house been cleared?' RJ asked.

"Yeah, we were out here yesterday. " RJ noticed two dog dishes sitting by the house wall in the shade, one was empty and the other was half full.

"Where are the dogs?" RJ asked.

"Oh, good question, I didn't notice those before."

The house rafters creaked in the silent pause of dialog between the two. The officers walked through the house. Junk and old newspapers collected thick in places about the rooms. More than once, they had to turn sideways to pass through.

"This is going to be a nightmare for the crime scene guys," RJ said.

The patrolman laughed, "We aren't quite as advanced on the science stuff here in southern Utah, as you guys are. Besides by all accounts this guy is a little off center. We aren't going to commit a lot of resources until we know we got a crime."

The best theory I have on my case is an illegal abduction," RJ replied, " so I would be very interested if you found any say... women's clothes, running shoes,etc....
since this seems to be a reclusive type guy. Or, for that matter please document if you find anything that wouldn't fit this guy's lifestyle."

"Good luck," the patrolman said," all you need is ten guys, a back hoe and about a week, you'll be done-or have a good start for sure!"

"Amen to that!"

They arrived with a roll of yellow tape that had POLICE LINE: DO NOT CROSS written at regular intervals down the length of it.

Jason didn't know any attorney's; in fact he knew nothing about law or legal actions. He did know he had just been evicted from his home by a couple of local cops who hardly knew their asses from a hole in the ground.

Quiet fury began to boil in him, the victim just treated as a criminal. The ground dropped from under him when the realization ran through him; if he didn't find Chiara soon he could go to jail.

The patrolman who had just finished the taping said, "Detective Jones will be in touch and you are to let him know where you can be contacted at all times." Then he slammed the car door in Jason's face just before the other patrolman sped away showering him with fine gravel.

Jason's first instinct, to pound the window with his fist, shriveled into nothing, along with the unedited roar in his throat as the realization he was now a homeless victim as well, fully engulfed him.

He was unsure how to proceed; he needed a place to stay but was too embarrassed to call Tommy or any other friends. His truck was the next obvious choice, but he was told to stay near a phone, so he decided to drive on down to Mesquite and get a room in one of the hotels. He would have to put it on his credit card because he had been jobless for the last two months; therefore penniless.

He drove up and down the miniature strip in Mesquite, searching for something cheap but decent. As he passed The Crown Jewels Casino and Hotel, the marquee flashed a special on rooms; thirty nine ninety five per night.

The casinos usually allowed better room rates, assuming they could make up the money on the gambling end of the patron stay over, Jason swung his pick up into the parking area and walked quickly into the lobby. He didn't want any of his buddies to see him homeless.

The sound of slot machines and casino action assaulted his nature oriented ears and he was immediately distracted. He felt out of his element. An outdoors person inside a casino is much like a wild animal abandoned on the downtown streets of New York City.

Holding his vulnerability close and silent, Jason avoided gawking at the scene of bells, whistles, lights and people smoking cigarettes non-stop as they waded into and sat staring at the hypnotic games of chance and hope. He shook his shoulders and closed his mouth and walked up to the front desk to get a room. He picked up the key and turned to search for the elevators before moving into the crowd of people.

The front desk was conveniently placed in an indirect line to the elevators; thus forcing people to move among the slots. Finalizing his intended route, he moved out purposely as a steady line of people moved around him. Unnoticed by Jason was a big square shouldered man in a black blazer, walking the opposite direction through the casino.

Jack had developed a photographic memory for security concerns in the casino and he just passed a face that he recognized. He stopped to look at a slot machine that wasn't being played, and then with as much subtlety as possible watched the back of the rumpled man who slowly but with intent, worked his way through the crowd. He had a day pack slung over his shoulder. Jason stepped into the elevator. The big shouldered man in the black blazer moved into a service hallway and spoke into the small microphone in his sleeve.

"Surveillance, elevator six, "Jack whispered into his wrist. Next he entered a service elevator and inserted a key into the lock by the flashing second floor indicator light. That floor was filled with rooms that housed sensitive activities and was completely off limits to the public.

He got off the elevator and walked down the hallway past nondescript gray doors. Jack pulled the key ring from his pocket and unlocked the door. He entered a room full of video monitors, which were manned by three technicians.

"Stevie," Jack said to a twenty year old black man with a shaved head, "I need an ID on the guy in elevator six."

"Already working on it, Jack," Stevie said.

"Is he a guest here?"

"Yep, he checked in as a Jason Bactiere. You know him?"

Jack's left hand closed into a fist but he kept his face blank.

"No, I thought he looked like a card counter from New Orleans; the one who took us for a cool half mil last year."

"No that guy was much beefier than this Jason guy," Stevie said.

"Oh yeah? Well keep your eyes peeled on this guy he may have lost weight. I want to know when he moves. Page me immediately," Jack said.

"You got it, Boss," Stevie said with a slight smile. He was quite relieved that Vinny wasn't around to harass them for a while.

Jack left the room and cursed silently. He didn't want to say anything to the techs but he had recognized the man from elevator six. It was the guy on television looking for his girlfriend who happens to drive an old yellow Subaru. Vinny's stupidity was coming back to haunt him again. This was the case that kept re-surfacing; increasing in complexity each time it came back. He got off the elevator on the tenth floor, and walked to Joey's office.

Joey's receptionist, Vanessa greeted him, rumor had it that she did her best work in the office after hours, but Jack avoided the rumor mill especially when it involved the boss. It was in his best interest to appear to be the loyal solider. Joey summoned him in.

"What a day, huh Jack, I'm not sure I'll ever get used to this heat, one hundred degrees, and I thought the summer was over,"Joey said, " a few years back I tried to relocate my mother out here, but with this heat she will never move out here."

"The temperature isn't the only thing that's going to ruin your day, Mr Scapalini."

"What now Jack!"

"That car I moved from Bruja canyon, that girl's boyfriend just checked into the house. I recognized him from the new's bit the other day.'"

"Could he know the car is here? Is there any way he could have followed you from the canyon?"

"There definitely wasn't anybody out there when I went out with the box truck. I had my night eyes on, and I moved very slowly," Jack said a little defensively," I know what I'm doing."

"Fix this Jack;I pay you to take care of these things."

"I'll take care of this."

Jack left the office and passed Vanessa without saying anything. He left the office and passed Vanessa without saying anything. She watched him walking down the hall, enjoying the show, and thought that she might like to work on that prize. Jack was pissed off, Joey was always so careful to never give a direct order. He always kept to the plausible denial dialogue so he could beat a wrap if anything came down.

CHAPTER 17

The morning dawned without incident; Chiara had slept through the night with Isa curled up behind her. Chiara felt change in the air; two days ago she had seen high flying cirrus clouds cross her small sky-gap in the canyon.

As the breeze picked up she realized the air was hot; unusual this early in the morning. She wondered if bad weather was headed her way. She moved to look for a protective overhang, in case of rain.

She paced the canyon like a nervous cat. Escape from here would have to reach a resolution soon. Stopping at the plunge pool she bent down and drank; as she stood a great wave of weakness flooded her veins.

The water, while keeping her alive had also given her a nasty case of diarrhea. Combined with the lack of food, she was now forced to deal with episodes of extreme limitation and she even felt lightheaded. Each time she sat down to rest, Isa would come near to lick her arm or hand, as if to heal her wounds.

Isa had buoyed her courage the past few days, but as Chiara faced the final possibilities, her fortitude lagged. Just when she thought she had overcome the worse; the next survival challenge bumped her back to ground zero.

Over time she came to love the little canyon; it's various moods and colors that fluctuated within the day, lent an intimacy that comforted Chiara through this perilous time. If she had to die; she reconciled that Bruja would be an honorable mausoleum. No other human would connect to this place in the same way. At least she hoped for their sake, they wouldn't have to. This Bruja canyon had definitely bewitched her.

Chiara spent considerable time during this isolation thinking about life; and especially all the aspects of her personal life. She came to several conclusions regarding the need to make plans if she got out.

First on the list included a reconnect with her mother. She had never known her father but she would make a concerted effort to learn more about him and her mother and their history. And then there was Jason. She knew he was the foot loose, fancy free type, but now she deeply felt life was too fleeting not to love fully each and every possible moment. This near death awareness motivated her toward a total and deep commitment to life; in all it's nuances.

She prayed; to God, to the creator, to the Universal Energy, to That Something Bigger Than All of Nature or to whatever anyone wanted to call IT. She begged that Jason's strong rock climbing fingers might once more; caress her face, stroke her hair, or hold her hand. The moment she saw him, smelled him, hugged him, she would immediately ask him to marry her. As a final point on her personal commitment to her recovery, she planned to find whatever medical care necessary to assist Isa into a smooth transition back into a healthy and enjoyable life as a member of their family.

The fall into Bruja Canyon had pushed Chiara deep inside her self. She recognized that nine days ago a literal fall into the earth had opened her on levels beyond conscious awareness. That fall had magnified so many parts of her life so she could study herself like she had not been able to do in the past.

The magic of Bruja Canyon had broken and bruised her body and bones; had forced her mind to let go, such that it would allow her to focus down further into the secret components of a fine-tuned soul.

"Yes!" she shouted to the now full hot sun. And that's when it hit her, "Maybe the sun is the true God. It was definitely responsible for creating the earth, tree's, animals, it makes the planets orbit and yes it is even responsible for creating humans, and even her. It was undeniable the sun was the great creator, and the early people worshiped the sun.

At last the pieces had fallen into place; a fragmented past melded into an illuminated mosaic that when viewed from the deepest perspective, became her radiating sunbeam center.

"Yes!" she whispered to the wind, with arms lifted to the sky. "What I see and feel and hear out there, is also in here! It is also in here," she said with her hands encasing her head.

Over the previous few days, glimpses of another future event floated in and out of her weakened consciousness; the start of a real family, something that she would never have considered before. If Jason agreed, they would add a child to Steg and Isa.

"Hmmm, such sweet dreams, we have." She muttered to Isa as she moved from the stone ledge and began yet another circle of her rock enclosure. The sunlight faded and when she gazed skyward, dark clouds laced the rim. The temperature, and her mood, dropped ten degrees.

Still confused about why someone hadn't found the car and come looking for her; maybe the note lent utter cause for them to wonder about her motives. She'd been known to utter the suicide word during the years with her mother; surely Jason had called her mother as soon as he realized she was lost.

Panic stirred the darkness that fluttered and fanned deep inside Chiara in tandem with brooding skies above her. Someone must have come up to Bruja canyon to go hiking and seen her car by now. The car should have triggered a search by now. What if no one came for another month. Her mind raced into the horror.

Dried and cracking feet carried her once again to the pour off below the pool. The option of a jump waited beneath the menacing sky. She didn't know why searchers hadn't found her yet. The heavy realization that she stood at the precise moment to take matters into her own hands, stopped her breath for a full five seconds. With no air in her body she slumped forward and she locked her knees just before her arms slid down her legs. Then the tingling of fur on her leg made her eyes pop open and there was Isa standing in front of her gazing up at her face. She gulped a lung full of air and then dropped down to her knees embracing Isa with a long hug.

Still she stood upright and said, " Okay I have to do this now.... But what about Isa.

Tears flowed freely from her eye's. Would the dog feel abandoned by her, or would Isa follow her over the jump.

"And if you don't, and I have survived the jump to come back and rescue you. Could we find each other after the jump? I need you more than ever now,Isa!" she wailed.

She laid back down on the pour off with Isa sniffing around her, she studied the landing once more; it would be very difficult to control where she would land. The good landing places on soft sand were few, and scattered. Numerous large boulders had fallen out of this slot canyon over the millennium.

She found a modest strip of sand behind her that would allow her a few practice runs. Near the leap off place, she found enough space that would allow for a few practice runs. She might be able to clear the boulders below. She tried a practice run, but Isa thought she was playing a game and got in the way causing her to stumble. Her ankle, just beginning to recover from the fall, twisted into a searing pain and immediately throbbed. Thus a new dilemma transpired.

What could she do with Isa to make this a successful escape she wondered? If she pushed the dog off first, would she be able to live with herself? She could't stand the idea of hearing the dog scream in pain, if she hit the rocks instead of the sand. And now with her throbbing ankle, she wondered if she had the stenght to push her off in the first place.

The chances of the two disappearances being connected were slim but RJ made the call anyway.

"FBI. This is Agent Mann," said the voice on the other end.

"Hi, this is Detective Robert Jones, with the Arizona State Police. I'm working on a case here in Littlefield, Arizona. It's a disappearance of a young woman, who the boyfriend
says, went for a run. The reason I've called you Agent Mann is because another disappearance has occurred about one hundred miles north of here and I think there may be a connection but I can't get involved in that one because it's across state lines," RJ said. Orville Mann was a fifty year old FBI agent with twenty years experience chasing bad guys around the entire country.

Agent Mann, as he preferred to be called, stood by his desk listening to the detective. His shoulders were sloped as if the weight of the world were pulling them down. He was the Special Agent in Charge of the Organized Crime Division of the FBI centered in Las Vegas, but focused on the entire southwest. He was stationed in Las Vegas five years before with the expressed purpose of finding any remaining vestiges of organized crime. Las Vegas was very interested in changing it's image in the public eye and it welcomed the increased scrutiny.

He had the standard flat top hair cut that had grayed several years before and always wore suits that were in shades of gray or black. In the standard of the nineteen fifties he only wore white shirts but had recently began experimenting with color in his ties. In fact, today he sported a blue tie, but several times inspected it in mirrors, fearing that it may be decreasing his masculinity.

"Well Detective, we would be very interested," Agent Mann said removing his glasses from his face and popping the ear piece in his mouth, "we've been investigating disappearances very aggressively in the past five years, and two disappearances in one week within a hundred miles of each other, should raise some eyebrows." The FBI had been under a lot of scrutiny since the incidents at Ruby Ridge and Waco, Texas. The lead agents in all offices were on pins and needles and didn't want to leave any stone unturned.

"You could start in Littlefield and then move to the site west of St. George, Utah," RJ said, "I've looked around the second site but nothing in depth."

"Has any crime scene work been done?"

"Our reams are tied up for a few days but I've got it scheduled."

"No a couple days, is too long, if we're going to get involved, I'll have one of our teams up there in three hours."

"Sounds good," RJ said.

"Will there be any jurisdictional problems?"

"I've run it by my Captain, and he's given me the green light."

"Excellent, I'll contact the people in St. George."

"RJ, then added, "The Littlefield site has been cordoned off as a crime scene and we have around the clock security on it."

RJ spent the next fifteen minutes giving Agent Mann the details and location of the house in Littlefield. Within an hour the FBI team was assembled and en route. RJ met the team at the house in Littlefeild and the search began. Agent Mann, RJ and two crime scene technicians poured over the house, taking samples of everything. RJ had told them about the tee shirt and they made an especially careful inspection for blood evidence.

They used Luminal in the kitchen, bedroom and bathroom. The Luminal, is a chemical that highlights blood evidence and had a lot of hits in the bathroom.

Blood spray patterns on the lower part of the bathroom walls and the swirling patterns of blood on the floor indicated it had been cleaned up.

They stripped the sheets off the bed and collected several glasses from the kitchen sink to acquire DNA samples. In the middle of the investigation Steg wandered in the front door and meowed loudly, offended by the intrusion.

"What is this?" Agent mann asked, after turning to look at the door.

"Pet cat," RJ said.

"Well that would explain all the black hair," one of the technicians replied, " It's pretty much everywhere."

"Tell me the explanation for the bloody tee shirt again," Agent Mann said.

"The boyfriend stated that the girl had a bloody nose and he helped in stopping that; therefore blood got on this tee shirt," RJ pulled several photo's out of his jacket and passed them to Agent Mann. The FBI Agent nodded silently trying to formulate a sequence for this event.

"Could the splatter patterns in the bathroom be typical of nose bleeds?" he asked one of the technicians.

"It's possible," the tech responded, nodding, "but it could be other activities also."

"How much more work do we have here?" Agent Mann asked.

"We're about wrapped up here," the technician said.

"Well let's head to the other site and see what's turns up," Agent Mann said.

" I have to warn you," RJ said ," This place is extremely cluttered, typical of reclusive living."

"We'll do the exposed surfaces first," Mann said, walking out of the house into the afternoon sun, "if we don't find anything connecting the two disappearances we'll keep digging."

"Okay, " RJ said ," I'm going to run down to the local station here and call my office and I'll meet you out there."

"Sounds good," Mann said, and then pointed to RJ with his fingers in the shape of a pistol, "Oh have your office fax the results of the DNA that you found to my office."

"Will do," RJ said then slid into the Crown Vic.

Mann and the techs finished loading the van and climbed in and drove to the highway to head north.

CHAPTER 18

Four and a half miles from the top of Bruja Canyon and nearly nine miles from Chiara's location one large raindrop fell on the desert floor; a tiny dust cloud spewed up a few inches off the deck.

A second later, another drop landed, two feet away, then another and another more frequently now. The randomly interspersed drops increased at about the same time the wind picked up in a tumultuous whirlwind of tumbleweed and debris. Like a sheet of frosted glass obscuring the vision; visceral sheets of rain water fell without abate. The emaciated twenty year old woman smelled the water in the wind and felt the storm moving in her direction at a moderate rate; swamping the dry desert with a wall of liquid as it came.

The lead story on the local morning news spoke of Chiara's disappearance and the same fate that happened to another person just one hundred miles north of Littlefield. Jason had awakened late and out of boredom, flipped on the television. The fears of serial killers stalking the area were prevalent on the anchorman's mind as well as everyone else. Jason had a sinking feeling caused by the assumption that his girlfriend was dead somewhere.

He quickly surfed the channels to see if any more news or details would be forthcoming, but the news had moved on to other stories.

His mind spun with potential scenarios and his stomach churned, but he decided that maybe food would settle him down.

He didn't feel like driving so was glad to remember a decent restaurant was down on the first floor across from the casino. Cameras, behind black plexiglass domes, followed him through the casino; in fact they had been following him since he'd left his room.

Jason grabbed a newspaper and moved over to an empty booth in the restaurant.

On the first page of the regional section of the paper he read the headline: TWO LOCALS VANISH. The story about Chiara and another person named Joseph Rains unfolded in several paragraphs.
A waitress approached his table and asked if he wanted to order breakfast, but Jason was so enthralled in the article he hadn't yet thought about what to order. Quickly he ordered an omelet and the waitress disappeared with a smile.

His attention back on the story; he learned the location of the second disappearance, and right away something clicked in his memory. The article described the general location of the second disappearance, and right away something clicked in his memory. The article described the general location of Bruja Canyon, a place he had climbed several times before. It eventually occurred to him the name of that canyon kept coming up in the various conversations he had been having with a variety of people. Bruja Canyon was the common thread in all these events. The waitress brought his breakfast to the table but he was much too distracted to eat right now.

"I'm sorry ma'am," Jason said, "but I have to go now. Can I get that boxed up?" The waitress left, she wasn't smiling now.

Two minutes later he was on his way back to his room with his Styrofoam box and a of cup coffee in his hands. He powered the food down and picked up the phone. He called the Littlefield police station. Marshall answered the phone and Jason asked for RJ, but was told that he wasn't there right now. He also placed calls to Flagstaff to see if RJ was down there, but got the same basic response.

Jason was clearly told to stay put, but the urgency he felt was too much to bear. He grabbed his car keys and headed down to the casino once again on his way to the parking lot. When he got to his truck he hopped in, but it was low on gas, he swung the truck back around and into the casino gas station.

Just as Jack walked into the security office, his pager went off. He entered into the office and Stevie said, "The guy from yesterday is on the move. He's down at the gas station, filling up."

He turned right around and then walked back out the way he had come and stepped through the garage elevator doors. He climbed into a sedan which would be less conspicuous then the Hummer when tailing someone. He swung the car out of the garage just as Jason was pulling out of the gas station.

Jack stayed back a safe distance, but didn't worry too much about being seen, because tailing someone on the highway is easy as vehicles often stay in close proximity for long distances.

Chiara savored the tranquil moment that always precedes pending chaotic energies.

Hanging full of liquid a sky full of ponderous dark clouds gathered. Supersaturated with tons of water near erupting, they seemed alive to her as if yearning to make contact with earth once more; to press and carve the will of the sky upon the prehistoric rocks beneath her.

Between the two powerful elements of nature, she stood calm and reed thin. Fully embraced by the smell of the forthcoming violence from the sky; Chiara reached a primitive level within her most sacred place. A thunder clap echoed up the canyon and the air crackled following the boom. Nothing existed for her, but the sky, the earth and the impending fury.

Was her life changing jump being supported by Nature's most profound elemental gathering? She had chosen a literal leap of faith. It was a powerful choice that would change her existence forever..

Faith that somehow she could survive the plummet into the unknown; surged in her blood. The echoes momentarily vibrated her soul; between the land below and the occasion above.

Peace surrounded her.

She understood that no one would come for her. If she were to escape this prison she would have to do it herself.

If she survived the jump she would come for Isa. It would be better than both of them starving to death together here.

Living a life of high adventure always on the edge of a great void in one form or another; Chiara would not embrace death sitting down. the void before her seemed a perfectly appropriate way to leave this world.

"Jason would approve of this decision!" She had thought of Jason often during her confinement; trying her best to choose what he would have chosen in the same set of circumstances. He was such a good climber though; he might have climbed out of here without breaking a sweat.

The sky held the impending deluge, but as the afternoon approached the breeze picked up to a definite wind. She looked down once more to the landing site, but it remained impossible to determine how much trajectory she could hope to gain.

"Let it go now," she whispered to herself. "be in this moment and let all thoughts go." Her voice seemed to be coming from outside her head.

She stood mesmerized for several moments; and then walked back up into the bedroom space to sit near Isa. She whispered thanks into her soft brown ear as she massaged the dog's neck muscles and scratched behind her ear's.

I promised I will come back for you, you MUST stay here Isa!" Her voice had a pleading sound, but Chiara wasn't entirely sure Isa would obey that command.

Animals had an instinctive fear of heights and it was impossible to know if the short time they had spent together was enough of a bond for Isa to give up her life for Chiara.

The veteran FBI agent was quite taken back by the look of Rake Rains' dwelling. "He hasn't thrown anything away in twenty years, " Agent Mann said.

"I tried to warn you," RJ said.

"Well you missed the bar, son," Mann said, he liked to refer to younger men as 'son'.

"I don't scare easily detective, but I thought you meant the guy was sloppy."

Agent Mann delegated the crew; the techs started dusting for prints while RJ and Mann moved bundles of newspapers and bagging items of interest. The elder FBI agent ran across a wall full of photo's of women.

"What do we have here?" Agent Mann asked with his eye brow's furrowed.

"The story I heard on this guy is; he was a polygamist and the state threw him in prison for keeping , like ten wives and a bunch of kids, so he became a recluse and the rest as they say, is history," RJ related.

"Hmm," was the only response Agent Mann uttered, rubbing his chin between his thumb and forefinger." He wondered what the attraction was to this lifestyle.

Then the agent walked into another room but RJ took a double take at the photos. Next he stepped outside and looked to the west; storm clouds had formed over the escarpment behind the house.

"We're in for a gully washer," he said to no one in particular, "hope this roof doesn't leak."

Jason drove to St. George then continued west. The sky didn't look so good to him either. He flipped on the radio to get some weather information. After fifteen minutes of oldies on the radio the disc jockey came back on.

"Hey kids, how are you doing out there in radio land?" the D.J. asked.

"I'm going to have a busy day here at the station. The weatherman is calling for a high of ninety-three degrees, and during my years in medical school, ha! I learned that the human body can't distinguish between hot and cold at ninety three degrees. So, people are going to be calling me all day to find out if they are hot or cold. Oh and by the way there are some thunderheads forming over Nevada so be careful out there."

Jack stuck with Jason although he knew exactly where they were going.

"How could he possibly have seen me take that car?" Jack said to himself, then reached into a bag next to him on the car seat and checked for his khaki colored clothes. A little further down the road, he pulled a gun in a holster out of the same bag.

"All this because of that asshole Vinny," he muttered. He felt the need to cut his loses while he had this opportunity. If this mess elevated to the next level he would have to leave this job and disappear.

As Jason approached Bruja Canyon he saw what looked like police cruisers parked in front of the land owner's house. Since he had been told by the detective to stay put, he decided to drive to the far side of the creek bed which would keep him and his truck hidden beneath the creek bank. The only hitch to this plan was the soft sand in the creek bed. He had to shift into four wheel low to make further progress.

The dust thrown up by Jason's truck was the perfect cover for Jack following about a half of a mile back. Jack saw where Jason had cut across and saw the reason for it, so he followed down into the creek.

Unfortunately for Jack, the sedan wasn't up for the soft sand and quickly bogged down. Jack tried to rock it free, but only dug it in deeper. His vehicle stalled a quarter of a mile from the mouth of Bruja. Jack jumped out of the stuck sedan, stripped his clothes off and put on his khakis; then strapped the gun around his waist. The ex-special forces commando was back in his element and he started a strong loping gate up the creek bed to follow Jason's tracks.

Jason saw the Bloodroot tree growing along the side of the creek bed where they usually parked for the shade. No sign of Chiara's Subaru caused an immediate knot in Jason's stomach He was stepping out of the truck when a flash of light caught his eye. It came from beneath him. Squatting down to the sand he picked up a small piece of glass that looked like automotive glass. Digging around in the sand he contacted and lifted a metallic object that he picked up and lifted up to his face. His stomach leaped up into his throat and the air was sucked out of his lungs. He recognized the hair barrette as one of Chiara's.

A thunder clap echoed up the canyon as if choreographed and the air crackled following the boom.

It was the barrette that he had given to Chiara as a birthday gift.

"She must have been here!" he shouted inside his mind. He wasn't sure what had happened to the car but he felt it wasn't good. The adrenaline rush filled him concurrently; with hope and fear. He had a strong feeling Chiara was still alive somewhere.

He remembered that she had mentioned, a couple times her desire to run the circuit of Bruja Canyon. He decided that he was going to find her; or die trying.

Snatching a jug of water and an energy bar, he took off up the trail to the plateau. He ran and continued back towards the west; searching every nook and cranny, as he proceeded up the trail. The sky began to swell with heavy clouds, but his mind was focused on the task at hand. He kept moving until at that precise moment, a great flash of horizontal lightning flashed the length of the canyon; followed immediately by ear splitting waves of sound that echoed both directions in the chasm before him. Bruja canyon had many side canyons that ran into the main canyon usually at a ninety degree orientation. At each side canyon the trail swung wide away from the main canyon. One of the first side canyons lay almost directly across from Chiara's canyon and if Jason would have looked over the edge just before the lightning bolt, he would have looked right into the canyon that held Chiara and Isa.

He felt her near him, but he didn't see her.

"Hey."

The word startled him from his complete concentration. He looked up but had to spin around and look behind himself before he located the source.

A man; a big man wearing khakis stood about one hundred yards behind Jason. Something didn't feel right about this, the guy wore a black belt around his waist that looked like a weapon. The khaki outfit had military written all over it. Jason was transported back to Saudi Arabia.

Jack out of breath from a quarter mile sand sprint, had worked hard to catch up with Jason. The young man made it clear; his shout was not going to deter him from his intent. He was like a blood hound on a hot track. Jack realized he had to do something to slow him down. He had chose to shout again to him and fake distress.

"Hey, I need a little help over here," Jack shouted.

Jason was about ten yards from the third side canyon and sensing danger not distress coming from the stranger; he turned and ran for it.

Jack was out of options now; convinced that Jason was on to something, he pulled
his gun from his waistband and shot twice just as Jason jumped down into the side canyon.

Jason was lucky, the canyon floor was only about a five foot drop but the shooter was trained with the weapon and the two rounds hit the wall about a foot from his leg.

Simultaneously, another thunderclap exploded across the sky, startling both men.The next second, using the distraction in his favor, Jason sprinted down the side canyon towards Bruja. He had explored this canyon and knew that he could probably circle back around to his truck and make it over to Detective Jones, should this crazy guy continue the shooting. The canyon was so tight that Jason bumped his shoulders along the walls as he ran.

Jack made it to the edge of the side canyon and looked in. Jason was no where to be seen, Jack ran towards Bruja and then looked down into the canyon one hundred feet below him.

Jason continued running downhill; back the way they had come up. Jack took another shot, which hit the canyon wall beside Jason; flinging rock fragments in every direction, lacerating Jason's face.

Jason dove under an overhang next to the canyon wall. Jack realized he wouldn't get another shot and proceeded to run back toward the head of the side canyon. Halfway back he jumped fifteen feet down into the side canyon and rolled to deflect some of the impact. The sandy floor of the main canyon descended steeply with three more five foot drops but Jason kept moving. Finally the last drop took him to a flat section of Bruja. Jason was seen by Jack at the lip of the last drop, but then disappeared.

Her stomach churned as she prepared herself for the jump of her life. The sound of another huge thunder clap startled Chiara in to action.

She gave Isa the stay gesture and then she did a practice run; barely limping to the edge. The excitement of the storm and her fear pushed adrenaline through her ankle pain.

Isa stayed put, but her ears perked up as she watched Chiara with interest. Chiara walked back and repeated the command word and signal. This time Isa sat and didn't move. Chiara almost ducked from the force of the next thunder crash as the sound wave finally made it's way to her; it seemed like it was right overhead.

She looked back at Isa who was now running in tight circles around the upper bedroom. The vibrations started off subtlety and then picked up to the point she could feel them through the soles of her shoes. It was as if the ancient rocks were humming with excitement.

Approximately sixty seconds passed as Chiara tried to figure out what was happening; at the same time tried to calm Isa. Chiara's heart was pounding at such a high rate that she didn't even notice the lesser pop's that were happening around her.

At that precise moment, a great flash of horizontal lightning rocketed across the sky with an almost immediate boom of thunder. Isa had a desperate look in her eyes and bolted even faster around the bedroom area space; since she couldn't fight this unseen danger, this was her version of flight.

Chiara ran to arrive at the edge of the pour-off just in time to see a wall of thick brown water come flying off the rim of another pour-off, in Bruja Canyon just upstream of her position. Tons of twisting water, rocks, cacti and other debris hit the floor of Bruja with a mighty blow. The supremacy and force of nature spawned a passionate and profound deluge.

Jason felt the flash flood coming before he saw it. He knew he had to get out of canyon, now!

He glanced up, then down the canyon to evaluate the path he must take. Just then he saw a round pocket in the limestone about fifteen feet feet up on the wall. and he caught a glimpse of a monstrous wall of water about to over take him.

Liquid so laden with mud it writhed like a brown serpent sinuously moving muscle tissue and vibrating the ground he stood on. At a distance it defied the fluidity of a liquid as it searched for it's next victim.

He became immediately empowered by the raging elements of nature.

The life saving pocket above him was one of many solution pockets in the sandstone wall. It was a common occurrence in this area. Jason had perfected a party trick over the years where he would run directly at a brick wall and using momentum and friction he virtually ran straight up fifteen feet of vertical wall. Of course, specialty rock climbing shoes assited his efforts.

If he could combine that trick with his dead point maneuver on this pocket, he might avoid the raging flood that threatened to suck him down, taking him to his death.

Jason didn't know what had happened to the attacker, but assumed the flood had taken care of that problem. He realized that hanging on the side of that wall, trapped by the flood, was about the easiest target that he could make for the shooter; his choices boiled down to get shot or sucked into the torrent.

The second he hit the hold he glanced upstream to see the guy who had been trying to kill him appear at the edge of the last ten foot pour off. The next second, a three foot wall of water took the shooter of his feet and then dropped him off the ten foot drop.
The water rose quickly but Jack recovered and was bobbing up and down; riding the current. He had dropped his gun at the moment of impact.

Jason clung to the hold with his fingertips as muddy water lapped at his feet. The canyon had the capability of filling quickly because of it's narrow width. As Jack approached, rising and falling on the rolling current; he spotted Jason hanging from the wall of the canyon and made immediate eye contact with his victim. Jason flashed back to the casino and realized he had seen this guy before.

Jack bobbed by his victim with a plan. With all the power he could muster he kicked his feet down; the power of his legs and the buoyancy of the silt laden water, shot him up out of the water just enough. He made a lucky grab for Jason's foot and landed a death grip on his shoe.

Jason felt his forearm tendons pop with the strain of the added weight of a dangling two hundred and ten pound hit man pulled by tons of rapidly rising water; immediately the twenty five year old rock climber was stretched out taunt into a forty five degree angle along the wall. Fully engorged blue veins roped around his forearms as an inner rage filled him; that a total stranger had such skill to capture him from the rushing water humiliated the rock climber. His fingers tingled and numbed. Nearing the end of his ability to grip; a fear flickered into his mind.

"Is this my nemesis? To be sucked into a raging torrent?" his mind screamed. His quivering fingers screamed back; and at that precise moment, before tendons could shred, an immense weight lifted from his hip bone. The shoe that Jack had grabbed finally popped of Jason's foot into Jack's hand.

Jason sprung up three inches. The powerful hateful pull had disappeared beneath him; into the turgid waters.

Jason's finger strength had endured the incredible strain on them. The stress on his arms had taken it's toll though. Surging brackish waves roared and leaped toward him. A split second glance downstream gave him one last image of the hit man sinking into the brew.

The joy of seeing that crazy guy disappearing into the muddy frothy flood was short lived because Jason's fingers were slowly sliding off. The powerful waters vacuumed him under. He touched the bottom within seconds, aggressively kicked off to bounce strongly and immediately upward to break the surface of the flood waters. He gulped a mouth full of air only to be pulled down again. Years of guiding experience taught him how to get in a sitting position facing downstream so he could use his feet to ward off approaching obstacles.

Chiara heard the roar before seeing the wave of muddy water charging down Bruja.

She stared dumbfounded at the volume, as the water flowed over the lip of the pour-off up stream from her; which was at least twenty feet from the boulders she had been studying these past nine days. Next, she watched a human head bob, twist and turn completely around as it went over the edge and into the plunge pool below.

"What?" she said in utter surprise. "What the hell was that?" she repeated.

She didn't see the head again until it resurfaced before the canyon turned around a corner out of view.

"Isa, who could that person have been?" The dog felt the tension rise in Chiara. She stood and then trotted down to stand pressing against her leg.

"Good girl, Isa. Stay now, until I can figure this out."

She stared downstream once more; to assure herself the person had vanished, then automatically looked back upstream.

Chiara's shock doubled as her eyes spied another human face; but this one had flailing arms. The person bobbed high in the water, but dropped back down again into agitated brown swirls just before the obviously-alive human rotated enough that she might see his face.

This person surfaced more quickly; as if he were an experienced swimmer used to powerful currents. She watched the head and arms rotate as he passed by directly under her. Chiara recognized something, she knew the face, and what convinced her was seeing the bicep with it's tattoo of thorns.

"Jaaason," she screamed, but the roaring water crashed around him to drown out her voice.

"Jason!" she screamed again with hands cupped around her mouth; then the man with the distinctive tattoo drifted around the bend without acknowledgement.

Chiara shivered in disbelief, "Did I hallucinate that Isa?" she wailed; then she shook her head. "No! I saw Jason!" she sputtered out in her excitement and nearly fell into the now raging river beneath her feet.

"They are so close Isa! Jason is just around that bend!" Isa wagged her tail furiously sensing the excitement. "We have to leave now!" She screamed, and then looked down at the boulders that were beneath her and had completely disappeared in a series of waves.

"Isa! Now is our time! Isa! This flood is our chance!" she was shouting now and Isa was barking. The rounded rocks disappeared quickly under the water and foam crested waves rushed over them. The whirling, surging liquid continued to rise swiftly as it pushed against the narrow-walled Bruja Canyon.

"Come on, Isa!" Chiara screamed to encourage the dog as much as bolster her own courage.

As the words flew out of her mouth the thin young woman jumped out as far as she could; and then fell into forever. Her feet impacted the water and she torpedoed down; but she didn't feel the rocks because the water had slowed her down and her feet barely touched them. Her thin body was quickly swept away.

The water was so full of mud that it was much more viscous than normal. Rolling and running waves bobbed her high; she was easily above the boulders but most importantly her spirit was free of that canyon prison. Chiara sped down the canyon and she felt relaxed and capable Then she remembered and glanced back up the canyon rim to see if Isa had jumped too.

Chiara had acted somewhat impulsively and hadn't taken the time to encourage Isa. Her loud shouting may have frightened the dog. She hoped her new friend would stay in the canyon because she was far from out of danger.

The water rushed both Chiara and Jason quickly and mercilessly toward the keyhole.

"You are on your own now, Isa." Chiara shouted to the blurring canyon walls. The canyon floor dropped a full five feet causing the water speed to accelerate. This incident cued Chiara to move from the animal caretaker perspective back into her white water survival skills mode.

Jason and Chiara had trained extensively and a refinement of river guiding skills from her Grand Canyon days, now played a huge part in her survival. Those lessons gave her a huge advantage in this crisis situation. She knew what position her body needed to maintain, in order to control the path she was being forced to take in this fast moving temporary, but deadly river.

Jason's voice echoed through her mind, "Stay calm. Point your back in the direction you need to go and then back-paddle with everything you have!"

Knowing that he was close by caused her to focus even more.

She knew the keyhole was on the right side of the canyon; now oddly peaceful in her mind, she worked her body with powerful strokes to the left.

The roar of the flash flood rocketing out of the mouth of Bruja Canyon quickly brought RJ, Agent Mann, and the two techs out of the house. The group watched as frothing brown and white water rushed out of the stone-walled gap; it was impressive even at this distance.

"Flash flood," Agent Mann said stating the obvious.

"I'm going down there, maybe some one needs help," RJ said.

"This is once in a lifetime!" one of the techs responded," Let's go with him!"

The group jumped into RJ's cruiser and drove down to the entrance of Bruja Canyon. There, they stood gawking at a ten-foot-high wall of brown water that twisted and rolled out of Bruja. It shot out of the canyon, like being shot out of a fire hose.

RJ noticed a red pickup bobbing up and down as it floated away on the flood. He thought he recognized the vehicle, but at this distance he couldn't be sure. The water once released from it's captivity, spread out across the flood plain, and then grew fifty yards wide as it shrank in depth.

"This is impressive,"RJ said, "I wonder if anybody was in that truck?"

"I'll tell you one thing I'm not going to find out, son." Agent Mann replied.

The four just stood and watched the mesmerizing magic of the force and the red truck.

"Amazing isn't it? If moving water can hypnotize people then a huge flood virtually captures them," one of the techs commented.

CHAPTER 19

The keyhole had been formed by a huge boulder wedged tight against the canyon walls but with a tight gap that remained under the boulder. Thousands of years of flash floods had packed enough debris in the hole that now it was just big enough, to where an average sized person could just barely squeeze through. However on this day the surface of the water appeared to stop against a solid wall and swirl gently.

Jack was confused by the sight of calm water in the raging river; then decided it might be a good place to climb out and swam toward the right side of the canyon. The flood waters surged again and a vortex created by the keyhole widened in size causing the whirlpool to grow immediately from two feet across, to four feet in total width.

The whirling pool looked as if it were draining out a huge bathtub. The scene was complete when a powerful sucking noise squealed up; as the air at the top of the keyhole was sucked down with the water.

Unfortunately for Jack, the powerful vortex was invisible from the surface of the temporary river; even at it's largest, four feet across and just as deep. The watercourse feature gasped open and closed; like the huge mouth of a hungry beast snapping in anticipation as the human approached.

Jack had never been a big water person. Choosing to spend time voluntarily at the ocean or on rivers was not a vacation option in his book. The uncontrolled flood rushed past him and into him.

Jack's rock hard stomach muscles seized as the moment of his demise was upon him. The vortex pulled him counter clockwise around the top; then swirled him, flopping him like a rag doll in a washing machine.

The fury of it all exploded in him as the lack of control overwhelmed him. He punched at the water with all the force his heavily muscled body could muster. The circular motion lowered Jack King into the monumental violence of nature.

All two hundred and ten pounds of solid muscle and worldly confidence was swirled and forced to face a terrifying experience beyond his control. Jack King looked into the black hole of destiny and knew he was dead.

The whirlpool sucked him down, feet first. The vortex disappeared over his head as Jack's body plugged the keyhole.

Death by drowning isn't always a quick death, but for Jack it was instantaneous; with ton's of water stuffing him into a rock hole half the diameter of his chest. The water, now without an escape route filled to the lip of the pour-off and began to plunge over the drop.

Jason worked his way to the left side of the canyon; working to spot another solution pocket, a plant, or even a cactus to latch onto that might save his life. He wasn't that lucky this time. He continued to float helplessly towards the keyhole. Just as he expected it to take him the whirlpool suddenly disappeared. The water continued to rise until it poured over the waterfall and with the water Jason dropped down to the plunge pool. The impact of this drop knocked him unconscious. He floated out into the calmer water out of the canyon, luckily for Jason, during the fall a bubble of air was trapped under his tee shirt and that kept him floating on his back.

Brown torrents sucked Chiara under the water again for what seemed like minutes but in reality was only seconds. She took a few strokes toward the light and broke the surface to siphon a breath of air and was taken down again as she went under another wave.

Surprisingly her calm continued, even as she was taken under the water. Freedom from captivity was definitely worth this wild ride. She drifted around the corner and heard another roar as she approached the final plunge.

Chiara dropped into the plunge pool but bobbed up because of her light weight. From her experience she knew the only way out of these situations was to dive to the bottom where the fast moving water would flush a person out. Terror overcame her as her brain envisioned the dangers of diving into the unknown; but common sense demanded relief soon.

Determination forced her to breath deep and long before she dived. Silent brown water rushed past her and Chiara relaxed into a float the rest of the way out of the canyon. She hadn't seen Jason since the jump and feared he may not have survived the treacherous water. She looked to the east while she drifted out of the canyon. Sun shone brightly across pressed azure skies; not yet crashed and cleaned by the monster thunderstorm that continued to brew far to the east. Weakness saturated her; muscles, bones and brain let go as seconds ticked. Chiara, too weak for any struggle now; let go and allowed the river it's will and way with her.

"So tired... I am soooo.... Jason where are you?" She whispered into the silent sky.

The rest of the team gazed at the canyon, as one FBI tech looked downstream. The red truck caught his attention and he continued to watch it's rise and fall in the distance, until he suddenly saw a human head slowly pass their position.

"I see a person!" he said. This FBI tech had previous Coast Guard rescue swimmer experience. He ran toward the bank.

"I've got him!" He ran down the bank, jumped into the river and swam out to the body but Agent Mann yelled for him to cease and desist.

The tech continued his rescue attempt and brought the man onto the shore. In spite of the agents directive, the rest of the group went down to help him get the man out of the water. As the agents worked on getting the man out of the water, RJ realized he looked familiar;

even though a person prone and soaking wet, looks considerably different than when they are standing and dry.

"Holy shit, this guy is Jason Bactiere," RJ said.

He looked up from the limp man just in time to see another person drifting down the canyon toward them. As the person floated in close to the bank, he jumped up and waded six feet out into the current to collect the second person. The realization of what just happened stabbed him in the gut. This wasn't just any person; this was a living ghost. His head spun just slightly as he reached out to grab her.

Weak but still conscious, RJ bent down next to her after the team carried her up onto dry land.

"Are you Chiara?" he asked. She coughed a few times, then said, "Yes, yes I am."

"How are you feeling?"

Overcome by emotion and unable to speak; the young soggy woman reached trembling fingers up to lips that quivered too as her fragile body sobbed and her eye's glistened with tears. Deep sobs forced air into exhausted lungs and mixed emotions first of defeat and then of sadness, but at the sight and of Jason lying next to her on the bank, she knew only unadulterated joy!

But seeing the tech performing CPR, crushed Chi, her love lay lifeless, next to her.

Her life saving experience somehow buoyed her and she crawled over to Jason, as she hovered over him, her tears splashed on his face. Then she wrapped her lips around his. After two or three breaths, Jason started coughing, and color returned to his face. Then Chiara collapsed.

Another gagging cough and the tech rolled her boyfriend immediately over. And began to assess him in case more advanced care was required.

Agent Mann walked back to RJ's cruiser and after fiddling with the channels on the radio found the local emergency frequency that would allow him to call for immediate ambulance response.

CHAPTER 20

Time spent working as a staff member in a hospital conveys a totally different experience than if passing through the same halls as an ER patient.

Staff are trained how to process sequential steps; objectively, precisely and as quickly as possible. Life or death can be determined by increments of lost seconds or minutes. Medical personnel are trained from the beginning to leave emotions, which cause disruption in logical thinking, at the door. As a result the patient becomes one of many people that need care within the emergency system.

Medical knowledge of and experience with the hospital staff left Chiara with certain medical apprehension. The ambulance ride from Bruja Canyon into St. George hospital strapped securely to a spine protecting backboard imparted little comfort or reassurance to the physical or mental mood of the young nurse.

Paramedics had placed Jason on the cot beside her for the ambulance ride into town and she was grateful to be able to touch him at will. Chiara, aware enough to hear his vitals sign were within normal limits but became concerned when her boyfriend demonstrated a lack of full awareness of his circumstances by asking the same questions over and over. She wasn't sure if he even understood that she was next to him.

Often, she reached over and to reassure and remind Jason where he was and why. Her nurse's training had revealed that repetitive questioning after a head injury often indicated a concussion. She had not considered that Jason might be injured while enduring her own fall from imprisonment and that wild ride to freedom.

Her ten day journey began with a free flowing run; now twisted to a surreal ride to freedom. The swing-and-sway bounce of the emergency vehicle mixed with thoughts of their future. He was now finally within her reach but in confused pain.

A multitude of thoughts and emotions undulated from her belly down her back as she sorted out her jumbled thoughts.

Where was Isa. Did she jump or stay in the canyon? If she jumped did she make it?

Did Jason sustain permanent damage in his attempt to save her?

Silent tears slipped down her emaciated cheek bones to infuse the rolled up cotton towels intended to keep her head and spine completely immobile. The ambulance sirens announced their arrival. Waiting hospital staff pulled open the ambulance doors before a complete stop; the back of her head throbbed toward unbearable.

Chiara knew the ER sequence; She knew the steps of the ambulance arrival upside down and backwards; lab tests, x-rays, Lactated Ringers I.V. solution through a line into her vein, and definitely a scan of Jason's head.

Nine day's of fasting had removed a substantial amount of weight from her small frame; hip bones protruded like outriggers. Her mind spun and continued to spin as the ambulance came to a stop. And that dizziness increased ten fold as the attendants whisked her down the halls on the gurney.

The EMT from the back of the ambulance had done the same for Jason as well as attaching him to the cardiac monitor. The regular beep, beep calmed Chiara's own heart rate; but still she couldn't fully relax. Amazed that Jason lay within a couple inches of her finger tips; was it only a dream? They spent five hours in the E.R. before being transferred into a hospital room for an undetermined amount of days.

The day Chiara and Jason were flushed out of Bruja Canyon was a busy one for RJ and it didn't end until late that night. He had skipped dinner and went right into the investigation. He recruited ten officers from the surrounding jurisdiction and Mann had called for five guys to come up from Vegas. Not much had been accomplished that afternoon and night, but Chiara had reported two men in the canyon; one being Jason.

The search continued for the unidentified man. Jason hadn't been much help that first night, so they fanned out downstream searching the banks of what used to be a dry creek bed but now flowed with a small amount of muddy water.

The two missing vehicles were relatively easy to find; they had washed downstream about two miles and got stacked up in a bend of the river. A wrecker had been called and the two vehicles were winched out. The windows had broken from the force of the water and debris and both vehicles were filled with mud.

Upon arrival, Agent Mann assumed control of the situation and asked for a bullhorn. A search team member dug one out from the back of a pick up and handed it to him. The agent stepped right into his element; immediately delegating people to go in every direction. He had them truck the vehicles to the FBI lab in Vegas.

RJ was assigned to follow the ambulance into the hospital and hang out with the two victims. His instructions were to glean as much information as possible and relay it back to the scene when possible. That order was only partially useful because both Jason and Chiara fell asleep within a couple hours of getting settled into their rooms.

He did talk to Chiara in the ER for a few minutes and she told him the story of the dog which made him walk away shaking his head. This story got more bizarre by the minute but he promised her he would pass the word on to the searchers to keep their eyes open.

RJ finally got a couple hours of sleep slumped in a chair in one of the waiting rooms.

Initially placed in different rooms; within a day the hospital staff realized that traffic control between the rooms of "local celebrities" could be eliminated if they occupied the same room. The exhausted young couple soon became overwhelmed by the constant influx of people; cops of all different description, doctors, Chiara's mother, up from Mesquite, climbing friends and other friends. Each entered the door with a look of amazement and some confusion. They had all started the grieving process and none really believed they would ever see Chiara alive again. Visitation became strictly controlled once the newspaper reporters and news crews began to arrive on the second day.

Chiara had not truly rested within the comings and goings of the various visitors; that people assumed Jason was somehow responsible for her accident and captivity in the canyon, appalled her. She wanted to reassure him and each bit of quiet time she made an attempt to start a personal conversation between them regarding their relationship; but each opportunity was thwarted by yet another walk-in visitor. She finally gave up and in quiet times the tensions collected silently in the room.

As Jason's mind began to clear, the hospital stay evolved into a nightmare, unlike any he had known. His girlfriend of more than a year had disappeared and he had spent days searching for her and trying to convince the authorities he knew nothing of why she had disappeared. He was suspected of murder, and then some guy he didn't even know had tried to kill him. He had been caught by a flash flood that nearly killed him; yet when he awoke in a hospital bed, Chiara lay right next to him. Bits and pieces of his memory came wandering back and seemed to repair, one-by-one, small pieces of that nightmare. The doctors called it something like post concussive syndrome; with a touch of post traumatic stress disorder thrown in for good measure.

Chiara, the cops, the doctors and nurses tried to explain it all to him; but he wondered if any of them really knew how to explain a process like that to anyone? In the end, the memories bubbled up into his conscious mind on their own.

Full of flowers, balloons, cards and all the trappings of sympathy and get well wishes; the room was all a bit much for a guy that thrived on the solitude of remote wilderness areas. He needed alone-rewind time; but this experience forced him to accept and identify emotions as they surfaced.

He had faced his mortality more than any other time in his life. His stoicism crumbled under opposing emotions that overwhelmed him on occasion. Potential loss sucked the air from lungs that yearned for big space and clean air; tears of gratefulness released the menace of what might have been. The reality of this event kept the strain and release of life; like the ebb and flow of ancient seas onto unforgiving rock.

The last nine days continued to wear him down like the ballet of rushing water over sandstone. Bruja Canyon continued to carve into Jason's recognition of true wealth; something familiar and precious inside that connected him to Chiara.

Most confusing for Chiara were the law enforcement dimensions; daily visits and questions about every detail of what she had seen and experienced, especially on that last day. It seemed unusual that such interest was made over a single woman getting lost for nine days.

Finally, when Jason went for a follow-up CAT scan, Chiara found an opportunity to ask a few questions of her own. She spoke with the FBI agent in charge, Agent Mann. He was a relic straight out of the fifties; a curious combination of Sergeant Joe Friday and General George Patton.

"Agent Mann," Chiara asked, "Why are you guys so interested in all this? I fell into that canyon on my run. It was an accident."

"Ma'am, after you and Jason washed out of that canyon, two more bodies were found in or below that canyon. They were dead." Agent Mann emphasized.

"Two dead bodies?" Her voice quivered with shock.

"Ma'am. After you disappeared, a reclusive sort of gentleman also disappeared. He lived near the canyon that you fell into," Agent Mann answered.

Chiara was silent.

"We wondered if the two disappearances were connected. That's why we just happened to be there when you washed out. We were investigating his house.

"Was he killed by the flood?" she asked.

"Well that's for the crime scene guys to figure out; but he had a couple of bullet holes in him." The visual of two bullet holes in a stone cold body stunned Chiara. Suddenly she understood why vigorous and constant questions were asked by so many, and why she was found coming down the same canyon.

"Who killed him?" she asked.

"That's what we are investigating, ma'am."

As an after thought the agent blurted out, "So you had a dog in the canyon with you, but you didn't have a dog before you fell into the canyon?"

"Yeah I know it sounds crazy, but it's true

Chiara trembled. Fear choked her throat as thoughts of what had happened to Isa pounded thru her. Could she have made it out of that canyon. She didn't mention her feeling for Isa to the agent. To every one else Isa's existence was just a minor side bar in this jigsaw puzzle. But to Chiara this was a major part of the story, and her mood dropped dramatically.

"Well ma'am, that's all the question's I have for you today, anything else you need to know?"

Chiara just shook her head, holding back tears. She simply took the card and nodded as he left, gazing at the floor.

Jason returned from the CAT scan and immediately; she told him the news that she had learned from the FBI agent. Tears welled before she got Isa's name past her lips. She couldn't explain the sense of loss she was going through.

Jason, still weak, stumbled out of his bed as fast as he could in spite of the tape, sheets and tangled tubes. He wobbled to her and the moment his fingers contacted her skin; a deep and spontaneous sigh escaped her.

Her pulled her gently close, to hug her long and hard;like he would never let go. Silent sobs of grief and deep relief surged through Chiara; she nuzzled his neck and relaxed completely into his circling arms. Jason's heartbeat pulsed strong and fast under her ear. A moan passed between them. Chiara thought how close they had come to never knowing this feeling again but there was always this scared space that they always could go. And she knew this was starting a profound and enduring relationship built of the fire of near disaster.

CHAPTER 21

The day after the ambulance had carted off the young couple to the hospital the search started in earnest for the reclusive man, at the scene of the flood.

Mann called in more FBI support crews during the night and by first light, dozens of searchers, two search dogs, a helicopter, along with several four wheel drive vehicles had arrived. By mid morning, they had all parked in bunched groups at the entrance of Bruja Canyon.

Mann remained in charge of directing all teams; however someone had made the bullhorn disappear, to everyone's great relief.

The river had dropped almost as fast as it rose and in the morning light the teams stretched across miles of desert; unable to estimate how far the flood might have scattered evidence. By two in the afternoon the canyon started to spit out evidence. Agent Mann's pace became frantic; like a six year old at Christmas. He appeared unsure of what needed to happen next.

A team of agents had rappelled into the slot canyon that had trapped Chiara and found it to be pretty much as she had described it. There was evidence that an animal had been there but no dog was found. That same team continued the descent down to the main part of Bruja Canyon which led to a grisly discovery.

At the next drop off, below where Chiara had been trapped, a human corpse had implanted itself into the canyon floor. It's torso, arms and head were visible, but everything from the waist down seemed to be drilled into the sandy floor of the canyon. The arms of the body were splayed around the head as if fighting something off at the time of death. That horror pose had been frozen by rigor mortis during the night hours.

The body was covered by a thick coat of mud and required a forensic team before they could begin to exhume the body. Three men were on the scene when the forensic tech arrived. The four man team was unable to pull the body out; iron bars, picks and shovels were requested and Agent Mann waited for another two hours.

He ordered a couple of the men to rappel off the drop and look back up to see if they could see the legs of the body sticking down through a hole, the legs were still fully clothed with slacks and boots. The removal of the body evolved into a full day's work that took five men and a Come-a-long to remove the body. The body was unidentifiable to any of the team members and was hauled out to the mouth of the canyon staging area, before being send to the forensic lab in Las Vegas.

As the first body was excised, a cadaver dog signaled on a pile of driftwood a quarter mile beyond on the downstream side and now in a dry creek bed. Piece by piece wood was removed from the pile until a body was fully revealed. The second victim badly beaten up by the flood had also been shot more than once.

As those two bodies were shipped to Vegas, Agent Mann took time to remind the crews to stay focused on the search, "Assume there might be twenty more out there," He hollered across the wash. Night collapsed the ability of the search crew with no more indication of bodies.

Agent Mann thanked them for the effort and climbed into his cruiser to go and search for his dinner. The last shaft of sunlight momentarily blinded his ability to see the turn off for the road back to St.George; so he relaxed back to wait for the big orb to disappear. A last look around netted him a glint from the base of a creosote bush. Mann hurried out of his vehicle to see what sparkled in the sinking sun. A gun joined the pile of evidence that had gathered on his seat.

"That water laid evidence everywhere!" He mumbled to himself, reaching for the radio-mike. He wanted to let the lab know he was headed in with the loot.

The next day as results began to return from the lab, Agent Mann was summoned back to the lab. RJ saw this as an opportunity to leave the hospital and make a run back to Flagstaff to see his wife. While he was there he could collect Jason's belongings to return, since the case had taken a dramatic turn. The phone rang while he was opening the mail on his desk.

"Detective Jones, Agent Mann," said the voice on the phone. Agent Mann liked this guy. He still thought of him as a kid; Mann made a mental note to make an effort to recruit him for the bureau.

"Hello sir," RJ said. "How's the case shaping up?"

"We've had a major break through, detective. Because you've been on this from the start, I'd really like you to see it through to the end. Continuity, you know?" The Agent smoothed and dropped his voice, before asking the next question, "How long would it take you to drive up here tonight?"

"Sure, let me just run it by the Captain, can you hold?"

"Yeah that's fine," Mann said.

RJ was back in about two minutes and picked up the phone, "Agent Mann, I can be out there in about two or three hours."

"Make it two, Son. This thing's moving fast and that's why you have lights on that cruiser!" Agent Mann laughed.

"Okay, I'll be there, asap! RJ said.

"You can meet us in Mesquite, The Crown Jewels Casino in the parking area by the gas station."

"Got it," RJ said and hung up. He dialed his wife at work and told her he was headed back to Nevada because the case was getting bigger. He decided not to stop in Littlefeild to return Jason's belongings as he passed by, because he was short on time.

Chiara had more patience with the continual flow of different types of law enforcement and other visitors since speaking to RJ; the detective that had dragged her out of the flood waters . He had come by several times to wish her well and seemed elated that she had been found alive and essentially unharmed. He used these visits to make conciliatory comments toward Jason; explaining that good police work looks at every possibility. Jason could only recall a few details of what the guy talked about.

The previous evening, on the day of the escape when Chiara's mother arrived. Immediately when she heard the news, the tension in her stomach returned. She had felt the contention between them from an early age. Neither of them made an effort to see each other more then once every year or two, even though they spoke monthly on the phone; so the opportunity to examine the unease that lay between them never arrived. Perhaps it was partially due to Connie's constant attempt to make end's meet? This resulted in her working a lot; rarely available when her daughter needed her the most. Or the fact that her mother never said much about her father; even when Chiara would ask pointed questions.

In Connie's eyes, tears brimmed as she entered the hospital room. The last ten days she could think of nothing but how much she loved Chiara and how she could have been a better mother to her.

Hands held out, she walked directly over to her daughter then reached out for her. Chiara closed her eyes, and stood still allowing her mother's touch. Unidentified feelings from the distant past separated them. Connie squeezed her hands as a soft sob shuddered between pursed lips.

"Chiara, I..." the breath stopped in her throat. "Please Chiara. You MUST know I love you?" Gently, she pulled the fingers from one hand away from Chiara's skin to search her purse for a tissue. Her heritage dictated little tolerance for discussions of emotional abandonment issues. But she wanted to forget the past and restart the relationship with her daughter.

Chiara sighed with relief and resolve. The trembling fingers of her mother that held tightly ti her own, conveyed the sincerity and request for forgiveness that words could not. Her mother's gesture presented opportunity; Chiara silently took a small step toward closing the wound; but she knew it would take some time.

Relief flooded Connie and she made amends to Jason for not supporting his efforts openly and with full confidence in him. Jason took it all in stride; partly because he was vague on the details but also because he was still alive after all the wild and crazy events. Connie remained with her daughter for the rest of the day. She fielded "visitors" as best as she could, but had to return to work the following day. During her stay she became reacquainted with Chiara and realized her daughter had grown into a beautiful and mature young woman. It thrilled her to see how quickly Chiara's physical and emotional wounds responded to the hospital treatment. She became more comfortable with the idea that Jason and Chiara were solidly together and bid them a fond farewell upon departing.

Chiara and Jason supported each other through multiple interviews over the next few days. Their ability to heal was motivated by their need to be free of the hospital, news people and law enforcement bonds. Chiara focused on getting out of this bondage so she could search for the body of her dog. Jason was happy to fully support Chiara's desires and waited patiently for the perfect moment to ask her the question.

CHAPTER 22

Joey dialed Jack's apartment for the third time. It was customary for the sight of those well muscled broad shoulders to outline the office door as he got off the elevator. Just as he hung up the phone then radioed security, Michael answered.

"Michael, this is Joey."

"Yes sir, Mr Scapalini?"

"Michael, I haven't seen Jack yet this morning . Can you find him and ask him to come and see me."

"Yes sir." Michael hung the phone up and walked to the security surveillance room.

"Hey Stevie. You seen Jack?" he asked.

"Nope, I sure haven't. Let me scan the casino floor, he likes to make a cruise through it in the morning to make sure everything is okay," Stevie said.

"Mr Scapalini is looking for him upstairs. So if you see him, let him know."

" Have you tried paging him?"

"Yeah, I'm going to take a walk around the place to see if I can find him," Michael said.

"Okay dude."

Michael walked out of the surveillance room and made his way down to the garage. A few things seemed off; the the Hummer was parked in it's normal spot but the black sedan was missing. In it's place, another vehicle was parked with a tarp thrown over it. Michael pulled on the edge of the tarp. An old dust covered yellow Subaru was under the tarp. He walked around to the drivers' side and saw that the window had been broken. He looked inside to see that glass had sprayed on the seat and floor.

There was no sign of Jack. Michael returned to Joey's office to report what he had found. Vanessa buzzed the office door and signaled Michael in. And directed him back to Joey's office.

"Well?" Joey said.

"No sign of him sir, but I did find something unusual in the garage."

"What might that be?"

"There's a vehicle covered with a tarp down there. It's an older vehicle; one that I've never seen down there before. Oh, and one of your cars is missing."

Joey inhaled a drag from his Cuban cigar as he leaned back in the plush leather desk chair.

Michael waited, Joey leisurely exhaled a cloud of white smoke that curled up to the ceiling. He looked up at the ceiling as if to figure out a complex mathematical equation. Michael continued to wait.

"Michael I need you to do something," Joey finally said.

"Yes sir."

"This is very important, I'm not sure where Jack is right now, but I need that vehicle disposed of. What I am about to tell you is for your ears only; comprende' ? Do you know how to run a back hoe?"

"Yes sir."

"Good, I want you to rent a back hoe and go out to the desert and dig a hole, big enough to completely bury that vehicle; get it?" Michael nodded his head in agreement. "Then tonight, I want you to take that car out there and bury it."

"Do you understand?" Joey asked.

"Yes sir."

"And Michael," Joey said looking the subordinate straight in the eye for the first time, "No one needs to know about this. Let me know when it's done."

"Okay I'll take care of it sir," Michael said.

"I'm depending on you Michael."

"Yes sir."

"I don't want to know where you bury it, okay." Joey said with a frown, "But when it's done there is a big bonus in it for you."

Michael nodded his understanding. Joey waved him out of the office.

The security guard walked past Vanessa and down into the garage; his mind swirling with thoughts of what happened to Jack. Where did this car come from? And why didn't Joey get his brother back from Mexico and have him do this car burying thing. Was Vinny involved with Jack's disappearance? Michael got the hidden meaning of Joey's words and knew that it would be very bad if the police were to find out about the yellow car.

As Michael walked past Vanessa the phone rang. The front desk receptionist had called because the FBI was in the lobby asking for Mr.Scapalini. Vanessa put the call on hold, and then rang into Joey to give him the message.

The phone clicked off in her ear. Seconds later Joey walked forcefully out of the office.

A blue blazer security guy walked down the hallway followed by Agent Mann, Detective Jones, and two other FBI agents. Rubbing elbows with crime figures was nothing new for Agent Mann; he enjoyed handling it like a drill sergeant. Those of the criminal persuasion didn't usually stand for that kind of treatment. Mann often got the information he needed by pissing people off.

The security guard opened the door of the conference room and showed the agents in,

"Mr.Scapalini will be right with you. He left the conference room to stand outside the door arms crossed.

Joey stood in the surveillance room and watched as the agents walked down the hall to the conference room. Once inside the conference room, he watched as the agents milled around, and then looked out the window, covering an entire wall. He wanted to even the odds in his favor. He wanted to know what he was up against; how many they numbered and if he knew any of them. To his dismay, the lead agent was a guy he had met before. In the past he had come into Mesquite to check things out and see if there any connection between Joey the syndicate here in Nevada.

The agents scanned the room until they found the hidden camera. In the surveillance room Joey and Stevie watched as agent's face appeared directly in front of the camera distorted by the fish eye lens.

"I better get in that room before they start tearing the place apart," Joey said, "Block this camera but send the feed to the tape machine in my office." He didn't want the security guards to watch the action in the conference room, but needed to review the tape.

"Okay," Stevie said , reaching out to a switch which changed the image back to the casino floor.

Joey tugged at his jacket and straigtened his tie as he approached the conference room door. He nodded to the guard and turned the door knob. Four agents turned to face Joey as he entered.

"Whoa," Joey said with the look of surprise, "Bring enough reinforcements, I hope."

"Mr Scapalini," Agent Mann said, "Federal Bureau of Investigation. Nice to meet you."

"You mean nice to meet you again," Joey said, "You were up here last year; harassing me for no damn reason."

"That's right, I thought this place looked familiar," Agent Mann said rolling his eyes, trying to remember the visit.

"Have a seat gentleman," Joey said waving a hand at the chairs of the conference table.

The two agents that accompanied Mann took positions at the door with arms crossed. RJ and Agent Mann sat down at one side of the table. Joey walked around to the other side and sat down.

"What can I do for you gentleman, this morning?" Joey asked.

"Where were you three days ago, Mr. Scapalini?" Agent Mann asked.

Joey laughed softly than said, "Agent,uh, Mann is that it? Mann?"

Orville Mann nodded slowly; he had great disdain for organized crime. His work against syndicates was the crowning achievement of his career. This place reeked of the mob and he was eager to bring it down.

Joey chuckled again, "That's great, I guess you could say, you're the 'Man'."

Agent Mann struggled to keep his anger in check; losing it now would jeopardize this case, He was smarter than this hoodlum and he would bring him down just like the others.

"Agent, do you have any idea what it takes to run this place? I spent sixteen hours a day in my office putting out fires and thats where I was three days ago; five days ago, etc.," Joey shot back.

Agent Mann turned and motioned one of the agents forward. The agent handed him a manila envelope. Mann opened the package and removed a series of photos; he removed the top one and slid it across the table to Joey.

"Do you recognize this ?" he asked .

"It's a gun. Is this an ink blot test?" Joey said with a smirk.

"No, it's your gun."

"How about this?" Mann slid the next photo.

"It's a car."

"No it's your car."

"How about this?"

Joey recognized Jack even though the face was badly distorted. He had practiced not showing emotion in these kinds of situations. The disappointment of seeing Jack's dead body registered with only a slight grinding of his molars.

"That would be a dead guy," Joey said.

"No, that would be a dead guy, that was your employee." Mann growled.

"If you say so," Joey said staring Mann dead in the eye.

RJ sat expressionless and watched the two face off. The practiced control that Joey exhibited, impressed him.

"Help us connect the dots here," Mann said.

"Why do you think there's a connection?"

More photos slid across the table. One was of another dead guy that looked a lot like Rake Rains.

"Because, this guy was full of bullet holes from your gun," Mann sneered.

"You know Jack King had a bad temper, he must have snapped," Joey said casually.

"The only problem with that theory is the gun had two sets of prints on it; yours and that true-saint-of-mankind, your brother Vincent Scapalini." A long gap of silence, separated the men; each hating the other, each determined to win the stare down.

"Where is your brother, Joey?"

"He's on vacation," Joey said.

"Where did he go on vacation?"

"I don't know, so if you are going to arrest me, let's get on with it. Otherwise I have nothing more to say. You found your way in; you can find your way out." Joey got up and indicated the direction of the door. The four men exited.

"We'll be in touch, Joey." Agent Mann smiled and turned away.

CHAPTER 23

Jason and Chiara were both deemed healthy after five days in the hospital and discharged. Chiara's priority was to start a search for Isa. On the first full day out, she, her mother and Jason drove Connie's rental car back to the entrance of Bruja Canyon.Connie had contacted the hospital that she worked and let them known she was dealing with a family crisis. One FBI team was seen in the distance using a metal detector to search the creek bed and canyon for any remaining clues that might explain the floating dead body.

"I can't believe my car disappeared," Chiara lamented.

"Just be happy you didn't disappear," Connie said.

"I want to go back up to the canyon to see if I can find Isa," Chiara said.

"No way," Connie challenged, "the doctor said you were to go home and take it easy."

"But that animal saved my life."

Chiara started to head up the trail. Immediately a wave of light headedness washed through her; she leaned against a tree.

"Your mom is right ," Jason said, "You're not strong enough to do this, and my head is still spinning, too."

Chiara began to weep quietly and said , "I need to find her! Please help me find her."

"I promise, Honey. When we get our strength back I'll help you look for her," Jason said.

"Chiara why won't you believe that the animal they found is your dog," Connie asked.

"I don't know; I just have a feeling she escaped," Chiara answered. "She is so incredibly strong."

The two of them coaxed Chiara back to the car. Shoulders hunched and head down; she agreed to leave. On the trip back to Littlefield she sat looking out the window; face long and silent. Connie, concerned her daughter would drop into depression, knew she would have to get Chiara some professional help before disaster struck.

Back at their home in Littlefield, Chiara went into the bedroom to lie down. Jason sat trance-like on the couch mulling over events of the last couple weeks; unsure how it would affect the future of his relationship with Chiara.

The apartment had been worked over thoroughly by the FBI tech's so Connie tidied up for something to do while the younger adults got some much needed down time. Jason stared at the duffel bag with his clothes inside not really motivated to do anything with it.

A man walked his dog along the bank of a damp creek bed that ran out from the mountains and canyons to the east not more then a quarter of a mile away from the town of St.George. He watched the dog sniff along the creek; the animal alerted on a small pile of driftwood up against the bank. The man saw his dog signal and watched as the animal grew more excited by the second; tail up, circling the wood pile with a continuous whine.

He walked over to the pile and tentatively kicked at it. The dog barked enthusiastically. The man kicked again, trying to dislodge some of the wood. With a thud, he realized the thing he kicked was actually the body of something; he backed off and immediately went to a phone to call the authorities.

The local cops contacted the FBI team that were still working the canyon. The team came down to examine the body and discovered it was a dog. This fact was deemed unimportant until they realized this dog had been shot.

The FBI team contacted Agent Mann. RJ overheard the conversation and was sad to realize this could be Chiara's dog. He knew how strongly she felt about the dog and found the nearest phone.

The ring jolted Jason out of the trance. He reached over to pick up the handset.

"Hello," Jason said in a dull voice.

"Jason?" RJ said.

"Yeah."

"Jason this is Detective Jones."

"Yeah?" Jason said, the tiredness coming through his voice.

"Jason, I know how Chiara felt about that dog that was in the canyon with her. I'm calling to let you know the last FBI search crew found the body of a dog in the creek bed and I think it is probably Chiara's dog.

"Okay," Jason responded.

"How are you guy's doing?"

"Uh, you know, just recovering."

"Okay did you get your stuff back?"

"Yep."

"Well take it easy Jason."

"Thanks," Jason said and sat the receiver back on the cradle.

The strained look in Jason's eye's motivated Connie to walk over near him and ask, "More bad news?"

"The crosses seem to be coming in waves with no end in sight. I thought bad things came in three's. Now I think we're up to thirty three," Jason said.

"What is it?" Connie prodded.

They found the dog's body; now I have to tell Chiara," Jason said.

"You just did."

Connie and Jason swung around startled by Chiara's quiet voice in the room. She leaned against the door frame in a slump. Her eyes dry; having cried her self out the last couple of weeks. Nothing could surprise her at this point.

"I need to go there and say goodbye to her," Chiara said. Jason simply nodded, rising. He knew any discussion would be futile.

"I'm going to stay here and give you two some time together," Connie said.

"Thanks mom," Chiara said. She and Jason walked out and drove away in Connie's car.

The drive back to St. George was monotonous and silent for the first five miles. Jason had wanted to say something for the last couple days but between the whirlwind of activity and his sense of confusion, he'd put it off. The privacy of the car ride seemed like an appropriate time to bring up a subject that had been on his mind for quite sometime. He ran the different versions through his head.

"Chiara, these crazy last few days have got me thinking," he said and then paused for am uncomfortably long amount of time.

Chiara looked over at him and said, "Thinking about what?"

"When I thought I had lost you I felt devastation, abandonment. I didn't know how to face my day, and I promised myself if I ever found you again; I would ask you to spend your life with me," Jason said.

He held his breath; waiting for the response. The sweat beaded on his forehead. His eyes flicked off the road for a second to steal a glance at Chiara. A single tear worked it's way down her cheek.

"When I was trapped in the canyon I made a decision that I would tie up a few loose ends in my life. One of those unfastened details was the definition of my relationship with you," Chiara said.

Jason gulped. His Adam's apple rose and fell in his throat and he waited for more words from Chiara. She watched the bobbing lump in his throat as her own went dry and her body quivered with anticipation.

"So are you asking me something?" Chiara said, nudging him along.

"I am not really prepared for this. I don't have a ring at this moment, but I will get one as soon as we can afford it; but will you marry me, Chiara?" His eyes darted from the roadway to Chiara's teary eyes; watching him intently. "I don't need a ring and yes, I will," she said reaching across the car to place her warm hand on his forearm.

Next she slid over on the bench seat to plant a long and sensuous kiss on his cheek. For the second time in two weeks, the warm feeling of love filled her life. Jason's knuckles whitened with that kiss. His eyes never left the road; precious cargo aboard required his full attention, but he was on fire and wanted to throw his arms around her and never let go.

"Chiara! You just made me the happiest man on the planet! I love you!" he said with delight and reached over to hold her hand.

"I love you too, Jason I only wish that our joy could have included adding Isa to the family. Instead we are driving back to St. George to bury my good friend. I'm sorry....I am bringing down this festive occasion."

"It's okay Chiara I know how much Isa meant to you."

Chiara fell from the emotional high with a sigh. "This trip is bitter sweet. Thank you, Jason for driving me here. Thank you for loving me and supporting me as I love Isa the best way I can now."

Thirty minutes later they arrived at the entrance to Bruja Canyon. The FBI crew waved as they approached. They parked the car and walked over to the crew; explaining that they were there to see the dog that had been found. The lead FBI agent recognized Jason; he had pulled him from the flood. He stood; face beaming ear to ear, floating on a cloud that only saving a life can deliver one to.

The agent walked them over to a tarp where the animal had been laid out. They were about to wrap it up to ship it back to the lab. Even though the death of a dog wouldn't affect the case; it may add to the overall evidence.

Chiara knelt down and put an arm around the animals' muddy neck and hugged the cold, lifeless body; close enough to smear mud on the side of her face. Jason squatted next to her and put his arm across her shoulders, lifting the tarp to look at the dog.

"Honey, I thought you told me, Isa was a she."

Chiara looked up at Jason, thinking that the concussion was still affecting his memory. Her eyes followed his gaze down the lenght of the body. The roots of her hair tingled. This animal was clearly male.

Chiara stood, face pale. A tremble that started in her toes raced the length of her body and finally down to her fingers. She turned to walk two steps, and then stopped. Hands touched her mouth but then pulled them away once she felt the mud. She turned back; wiping the muddy fingers on her pants. Momentarily confused she walked back over to Jason, clutched his arm and said, "This is not Isa. She may still be alive!"

She looked around the area; there were so many questions from the last two weeks.

Where was Isa? What happened to her car? Who were the people killed in the flood? Who's dog was this and how did both this animal and Isa get shot? Chiara needed resolution; either Isa was dead or alive. She needed to find out.

Jason and Chiara walked back to the car and got in. They sat silently there for a few minutes.

"Now what?" Jason asked, looking for direction.

"Well, I am trying to think where Isa would go if she had survived the flood?"

"They checked the canyon where you were trapped," Jason said.

Chiara turned to the north and looked along the escarpment that formed the plateau above the plain where the canyon emptied out.

"Where did Isa's owner live?"

"Back down along this cliff about a mile."

Chiara wound the window down and asked the FBI agent if they could check the place out.

"Sure," the agent said, "we're done with the place."

They drove away slowly to the north until the ramshackle buildings came into view. Jason parked outside of the corral which amounted to Rake's front yard. They walked towards the shacks and wandered around the grounds.

Chiara choked up when she saw the large stainless steel bowl sitting in the shade by the house wall. It was obviously a water bowl for dogs. She had a vivid imagination of Isa walking around that bowl wagging her tail. She felt the presence of the dog, but didn't see her.

After an hour they decided staying was pointless and started driving down the dirt road. A dust plume rose; even though only a week had pasted since the big rain had soaked the roads.

The town of St. George bustled with activity. Both hungry; they decided to stop at a cafe on the main street. While they waited for their food, Chiara stood up and walked over to the pay phone. A phone book hung there.

After a few minutes she returned to the table and said, "The animal shelter is on a street named Bleaker Street. I think we should pay them a visit."

"Where's that?" Jason asked.

"I'm not sure." Then when the waitress brought their food Chiara asked, "Excuse me. Where's Bleaker Street?"

The waitress gave directions to the animal shelter across town. When they had finished eating they drove over to the shelter; situated down a dirt road near a trailer park. As they approached they heard multiple dogs barking and howling for attention.

The entry of the shelter also doubled as and office and a feline motel. To the left a wall of milk crates arranged in a way to allow access to each one; housed a large cat, some kittens and a collection of other cats in a wide range of colors. Several of the cats meowed as Chiara and Jason entered; as if pleading to be adopted. Most of the cat's simply hunkered down; afraid of the newcomers.

A young girl behind the desk stood; happy to see potential parents of one of the many adoptees. Chiara strode over to the desk with a look of anxiety etched across her face.

"Hello," the girl said smiling.

"Hi," Chiara said, "I've lost my dog and I was wondering if you may have found her."

"What does she look like?"

"She has a beige color and the hair that runs down her spine stands up vertically and is dark brownish."

The girls' face drained color as she stared at Chiara.

"Yes someone found that dog a couple days ago and brought it in," she said excitedly; than added with a darker slant to her eyes, "The dog was badly injured through."

"Yes I know, a gunshot wound had grazed her face," Chiara said.

"The vet just took her to his clinic. The truck just left! They do the euthanasia for us and he don't think she could lead a happy life without extensive medical work," she said.

"Where is the vet's office?"

"Get on the interstate going north; take exit 39 and drive about five miles and you'll see it on the left. It's called The Veterinary Clinic of St. George."

"Will you call them? Tell them not to euthanize her! We will pay for all her medical care!" Suddenly the girl realized that Chiara and Jason were the two people she had seen on television; the one's who had survived the flash flood.

Driving well above the speed limit put them into the parking area of the vet's clinic in ten minutes. Chiara bolted through the front door almost shouting for them to stop the euthanasia. In breathless spurts she related the story to the receptionist.

"Yes ma'am we got the call from the animal shelter, I'll show you were she is."

They walked through a swinging door into the back of the vet's clinic to enter a room with several cages. Isa cowered in a corner trembling. The whimpering began the moment she smelled Chiara walk through the door.

She stood up and was furiously wagging her tail when she came into view. Chiara opened the cage door and squatted down to hug Isa; now shaking visibly. Speaking softly to calm the dog; Chiara held her close The wounded dog had gained some weight, but the wound looked worse to Chiara. Jason was appalled by the facial wound..

The vet entered and introduced himself.

He was an older man; salt and pepper colored hair and a gray mustache graced his upper lip.

"Hello folks! I'm so glad you arrived when you did

"So are we," Chiara said, finally the anxiety flowed out of her.

"We volunteer our services to the animal shelter; it's a job we don't enjoy, but a necessary one."

Chiara just nodded her head still pressed against Isa's neck; she could feel the powerful muscles against her face.

"Can you fix this wound?" Chiara asked.

"I can suture the wound closed and give antibiotics but she may need to see a specialist to have some of the other work done."

"I want the best care for her."

"Okay, we'll get started then."

While the vet prepared the dog for surgery and Chiara comforted Isa the vet listened to the horrific story that Jason and Chiara related about the imprisonment and escape in Bruja Canyon.

CHAPTER 24

The two FBI agents that were posted at the Crown Jewels Casino and Hotel had a boring morning that extended into the afternoon. At six o'clock in the evening a new pair of agents relived the first two, the sun set and they settled themselves in for a long night. Then about midnight a large yellow rental truck arrived and drove around to the back of the casino. The truck was too large to pull it into the garage, so Michael parked it outside the door and went in. Within a few minutes an old yellow Subaru was driven out, up the ramp and into the back of the truck. Michael closed the door and pulled away from the garage.

The agents excitedly followed the truck and en-route to wherever they were headed, they radioed into the office. Before long Agent Mann was on the radio getting directions to their location, which was somewhat difficult due to the fact that the truck was mobile. Mann called for a helicopter and soon the chase was on in earnest. Once the chopper had the truck spotted he told the two agents on the ground to drop back but continue the pursuit following the directions from the air.

The truck turned off the highway, followed a secondary road for six miles and then turned down a gravel road. Two miles down the dirt road and about a hundred yards off in the desert was a back hoe parked by a large hole in the ground. Michael got out of the truck and opened the back door and only then did he hear the rotors of an approaching helicopter. Simultaneously, a vehicle, headlights off came speeding down the road and then skidded to a stop by a very stunned Michael. Out of the car came two men with guns drawn. Michael with a deer in the headlights look, put his hands up above his head.

Before the light of day Michael was in an FBI interrogation room in Las Vegas. The yellow Subaru as well as the rental truck and back hoe were also in the crime lab in Vegas. The chair made an obnoxious squeak as Agent Mann pulled it away from the table. The FBI quickly confirmed that the owner of the Subaru was none other than Chiara Martinez. Mann was beside himself with arrogance, this was one of those missing links that may connect Joey Scapalini and maybe more of the Scapalini empire with the deaths of two people. This kind of a feather in his cap was just what Orville Mann needed before his eminent retirement.

In addition to the Subaru, the head of Crown Jewels Casino security was found dead in Bruja Canyon, after trying to murder Jason Bactiere. Joey's gun was found in that area of the canyon's entrance and the bullets from that gun were found in one of the bodies and in a dog that belonged to the deceased man. The evidence was coming in at such a rate, the pace was almost dizzying and the FBI lab and office were scrambling to keep up with it all. Mann had needed one more solid piece of evidence to arrest Joey under suspicion of the murder of Rake Rains. Stealing Chiara's car may also lead to an attempted murder charge by preventing the rescue of the trapped girl. Now his task was to extract as much information from Michael as possible.

"Hello Michael," Mann said as he sat down.

"Look I don't know what this is all about," Michael said.

"Talk to me about this little burial ritual you were occupied in ."

"I think I need a lawyer before I say anything," Michael said.

"That's fine but I think you'll do a lot better if you make a deal with us, if you go to trial and lose you could be sent to prison for an unknown amount of time."

"Why is the FBI involved in this?"

"Because the car you were burying belonged to a girl who was stranded in a canyon and could have died, because no one knew where she was."

"I had nothing to do with that."

"Exactly my point, Michael, so why take the fall for someone who couldn't care less that you are here."

"Maybe I was just getting rid of a vehicle that was abandoned in our lot; I don't know how it got there."

"Well I have a stolen car, two cars destroyed, a woman who could have died due to someone's udder stupidity, one dead dog, and the capper of it all, two dead bodies," Mann said.

"As I said before, I don't know what you were talking about," Michael repeated, his face turning beat red and his jugular veins bulging from his neck.

"Think about it for a minute, I have a call to make," Mann said and stepped out. Michael sat alone in the interrogation room, wiping the sweat from his forehead back into his hair. He thought of how quickly Joey had moved past the death of Jack without even knowing what had happened to him; just another day of business. He decided at that moment he wasn't going to go down in this way. Agent Mann walked back into the room smiling broadly.

"It's a great day to be free, don't you think? Mann said.

Michael ignored him and thought this was nothing but an arrogant bastard, but that bastard seemed to hold all the cards.

"Well you want to talk to me or make a phone call and take your chances?"

"Okay, what do you want to know?" Michael said wondering to himself if he was just sealing his death certificate.

"Who told you to bury that car?"

Michael paused, knowing that once this name left his lips he would need to be put in the witness protection program. Then he sighed and said, 'Mr. Scapalini."

"Which Mr. Scapalini would that be?"

"Jocy Scapalini."

"Joseph Scapalini, and why would Mr. Scapalini want this car buried, in a place that it would be unlikely to find for a very long time?" Mann asked.

"I have no idea, he just asked me to take care of it and he didn't want to know where."

"Do you know Jack King?"

"Yes he's my boss, head of security at the casino," Michael said.

"Where is he right now?"

"I don't know, we looked for him this morning but couldn't find him."

"He's dead, one of the bodies that we pulled out of the canyon, a couple days ago."

Michael was very disturbed by this news and the tendons in his jaw flexed as he clenched his teeth. He had grown fond of Jack, a real warrior type but still reasonable, he was the kind of guy that would come through in the clutch. Michael couldn't believe he was dead. He didn't have any real information about the events that led to this but he had suspected something was up in the last few days, "You guys need to talk to Vinny about this stuff," Michael said.

"Vinny? You mean Vincent Scapalini?"

"Yep," Michael said.

"What would Vinny have to do with this?"

"I don't know but he was suddenly sent to Mexico on 'vacation'," Michael said making the symbol for quotations with his hands.

"Tell me some more about this," Mann said also making quotation symbols with his hands.

"You know I'm not very high in that organization but Jack hated Vinny and Vinny hated Jack, there was a lot of history there. I wouldn't be surprised by anything that involved Vinny, he was an ass."

"Okay Michael, that's all the questions I have for you now, can you stay in Vegas?"

"You don't think I'm going back to Mesquite, do you? I'd like to live more than twenty four hours, if at all possible. Which begs the question aren't you going to help me out with that?"MIchael asked.

"I'll take care of it," Mann said as he walked out.

CHAPTER 25

Impelled by little boy with blue eyes, Chiara planned a trip to the hospital where she worked. Her need to visit the young cancer patient and re-connect with her past. He was the last patient under her care before the life changing canyon event, and it couldn't be put off any longer.

She felt obliged to find out if he had improved; or to face the fact that his condition had progressed into the worst case scenario. The need to look deep and long into those blue eyes drove her desire. Her emotional connection to him in her time of need pressed her into a support position for him. The chance meeting in the emergency department had changed her life in a profound way.

Chiara had not spoken to her fellow workers for more than two weeks. She missed them and she missed her work. This last leg of healing required a reconnection to her professional life. Had her colleagues given her up for dead?

The walk into the E.R. was unexpectedly difficult. People hardened by years of traumatic human experience surged to greet her. The hugs and tears of relief resumed the bond of the emergency medical professionals. Quick to respond in unemotional ways; Chiara's return safe and sound allowed brief and celebrated respite among them. She felt love and acceptance.

The rapt audience listened intently to the stories of her experience and when the good news of her engagement to Jason was announced, they cheered. Tears glistened again and congratulations bequeathed her. An hour later the busy E.R. siphoned the hospital staff away.

Chiara left the E.R. and walked down to the gift shop. She bought a bunch of balloons and went up to the third floor and down the hall to the pediatric intensive care unit.

Would she find him on this floor, or somewhere else? The floor nurse directed her to his room.

She hesitated, smoothed her skirt. took a deep breathe and knocked on the open door. Chiara slid into the room and the child's eyes grew wide and a brighter blue than she had remembered in her dreams. His mouth opened in amazement. Chiara jockeyed the balloons through the door and walked into the room.

"Hi buddy!" Chiara said.

"Hello," a demure response came from the child; still unsure of what was going on.

His mother had been reading him a story. She placed the book on the side table as Chiara entered; then turned to the boy and said, "Do you remember this nurse?"

"She was on T.V.!" he said excitedly, pointing at Chiara, but looking at his mom.

"I was on T.V. Trevor, and do you know why I was on T.V.?" Chiara asked.

He shook his head in silence, his eyes still wide.

"Trevor I had an accident, and do you know how I got through that tough time?"

He shook his head again.

"Well, Trevor you are my hero and I thought about you during the really hard times and you got me through them. That's why I brought you all these balloons to thank you for helping me.

The next time she looked at Trevor he had a huge smile on his face, and the pride exuded from him.

She was glad he only had a vague memory of their first meeting, because he had a lot of procedures done and enduring all that tends to dull the memory. His head lacked hair, due to the chemotherapy after the surgery, and he looked way beyond his years.

Chiara pulled a brown teddy bear from under her arm and extended it toward him.

"This is for you," she said. He took the fuzzy bear and hugged it close to his face.

"And these too," she said tethering the ballons to the bedside table. A shy smile peeked out from under the arm of the fuzzy bear.

Joanne dialogued with Chiara about her adventure and while they talked, the child fell asleep. Chiara, tired of the story, and had begun giving the abbreviated version to people now. Twenty minutes later, the conversation switched to the child's treacherous journey through the treatment of his cancer; a journey that no parent would ever wish upon their child.

"Would you like to go and get some coffee," Chiara offered, thinking Joanne might need a break from her vigilance.

"Sure," Joanne responded as she pulled the blanket up around Trevor's chin.

They walked out of the room and Joanne cast a worried look back over her shoulder, then tore herself away. They walked down to the cafeteria, and then sat at a table with steaming cups of coffee. Chiara was curious about Trevor's treatment and recovery. she opened the conversation.

"You have a very brave young man there, Joanne," Chiara said.

'Yes, I know, but there is only so much a mind can take. He is so little and fragile." Joanne said choking up a bit.

"You know I wasn't joking when I said he saved my life. The first few days of entrapment I moved from extreme pain to shock and then into deep despair as I realized I might never be found. Through it all, those clear calm blue eyes kept reoccurring in my dreams. That vision became a life preserver for me. It helped me remain positive and to keep making the choice to never give up. The memory of his bravery focused me away from panic many times."

"I appreciate you saying that, Chiara. Maybe the fact he is so brave and helped you find courage through this struggle will do the same for me."

"How did he do with the surgery?"

"His official diagnosis was neoblastoma; based on what the doctors saw on the CAT scan and in surgery, and then of course the biopsy results verified everything," Joanne replied.

Chiara leaned forward; head propped up with her closed hands, then nodded as Joanne related the traumatic story.

"That must have been tough on you."

"When the doctor's opened him up they found tumors on each kidney as well as something on his liver which looked suspicious.

They removed the tumors, and then he was sent into the pediatric intensive care unit to wait for the pathology report results. That was tough; the waiting," Joanne said.

"How long did it take to get the report?" Chiara asked.

"Just a day, but it came back with bad news. The tumors were malignant. They decided the best course of action was chemotherapy to ensure there were no free floating cancer cells."

"I'm sorry Joanne," Chiara said swallowing the tears. She squeezed out a smile.

"He can still pull through this ; it's just so hard on him. I can't stop wondering why this is happening. He is so innocent!" Joanne whispered.

"I have very strong feelings that he is going to make it, through this," Chiara reached over to touch the mother's arm.

"Thanks, Chiara. Speaking of bravery though, your experience took a lot of courage. If it had been me in that canyon; I think I would have given up early on."

"Keep hanging in there; this is your canyon." The women stood and Chiara hugged her.

"And if you need anything, please give me a call," Chiara said. Joanne kept looking at the clock anxiously.

"Would you like to walk back to the room?"

"Yes, but really, thank you for giving me the opportunity to vent my feelings. I feel more able to handle things now," Joanne said.

They hugged again and walked back up to Trevor's room. Joanne took up her post as Chiara wished her the best. She walked to the head of the bed and stood there, a silent smile filled her at the sight of her sleeping angel. She waved quietly to Joanne and walked out.

CHAPTER 26

A sixty-something gray haired, sharply dressed man in an Armani suit looked poised and confident in the chair facing Joey sitting behind his desk. Thomas Bena was a high powered attorney known for the representation of high profile clients; he had represented Joey's father before his untimely and unexpected death. They laughed and joked about the old days in the 'neighborhood' when they ruled the roost.

Thomas Benatini had changed his name to Thomas Bena when he was in law school to avoid any connection to the mafia. After a law practice with a slow start and little potential business, he embraced the mob by revealing his true name and they kept him in business.

The buzzer on Joey's desk beeped just before Vanessa's soft voice announced the FBI. Joey thanked her as he looked at the monitor Stevie had recently installed. Now he could view any camera in the casino from his office desk.

He saw Agent Mann and two other agents outside his door. He flipped a switch and the monitor went dark.

"Send' em in, Vanessa."

"Yes sir," Vanessa said.

The door opened; Mann walked in.

"Oh, I hope I'm not interrupting anything," then pausing said, "Hello Mr. Bena or is it Benatini today?"

Thomas Bena nodded with a smug look on his face at the FBI agent and said, "Mann."

"It's old school day," Mann said.

"What's your business here Mann."

"This," he said, handing Joey a piece of paper.

"And what might that be," Thomas Bena asked snatching the paper from the agent, before Joey saw it.

"It's the arrest warrant for the murder of Joseph Rains and the attempted murder of Chiara Martinez," Mann said to Joey. "Your name is on it Joey."

"I have no idea what you are talking about," Joey said.

"Come with us, Mr Scapalini," Mann said as the other agents cuffed him and read him his Miranda rights.

"What kind of evidence do you guys have?" Joey asked.

"Well to begin with, Joseph Rains was killed by bullets that were fired from a gun that's registered to you," Mann replied.

"Joey don't say another word! I'll take care of everything," Thomas Bena said.

The group exited in convoy from Joey's office, passing Vanessa, who stood in silent shock and then on down the hallway. Joey was driven down to Las Vegas where he was processed; fingerprints, mug shots snapped, then interrogated at length by Agent Mann. Mann went through the majority of the list of evidence that had accumulated over the last couple of days piece by piece. Enjoying himself like a cat playing with his prey.

Joey held firm on the denial of any responsibility for any deaths or damage to any property.

"How did a gun belonging to you end up killing Joseph Rains and his dog?" Mann questioned.

"I guess I had a rogue security guard in my midst," Joey said, enjoying the confrontation with Mann; feeling confident now that Thomas Bena would have him out of there before the sun dropped on the western horizon.

One hour became four hours and still no sign of Joey's attorney at the FBI office in Las Vegas.

Joey grew tired of the cat and mouse game and clamped up; ignoring the barrage of questions.

"I want my attorney present before we go any further."

"I wonder what could have possibility happened to him. I remember, as we left your hotel, he said he would take care of everything. Maybe he's not as good as you thought." Mann chuckled and watched sweat beads break out on Joey's forehead.

"I'll beat this charge, even if I have to get an attorney straight out of law school," Joey responded.

"Not according to Michael Klein," Mann said.

Mann, skilled at interrogation saw a slight flex of the jaw muscles and knew he had accomplished both his goals with Joey; surprise and the edge of power he needed on his adversary.

"What did Michael have to say?" Joey asked.

"He told us the major points that we needed to know; but we need you to fill in the gaps."

"You guys are fishing."

"Now's your chance to cooperate, Joey. You keep playing stupid and we WILL be pushed past the point of no return," Mann said.

"Fuck you!" Joey's voice boiled with anger and frustration.

Joey was loaded in the paddy wagon, driven an hour out of town, and processed into a bright orange jump suit; the feel of the durable polyester against his bare skin rolled his stomach into a queasy knot. Large black NELLIS FEDERAL PRISON letters were stenciled on his back. He'd hit the big time now.

Shown to a holding cell in the prison; he sat down immediately on the vinyl covered foam pad that they called a mattress. He needed to think through this problem; how did things fall apart so quickly?

Jack was dead? Rake rains was dead? But Vinny was still in Mexico! Too many details were pointing to him.

Hours later, Thomas Bena arrived at the prison. Joey was shown to the conference room. A sheet of clear polycarbonate two inches thick, separated them. They communicated with a phone. Joey jerked the phone off the wall the moment he saw Bena's face and shouted, "Where the hell have you been?"

"Things out here are more complicated than they were back in Atlantic City. You must go before a judge before bail is set and can be posted."

"Get me out of this piss hole! You know I can cover the bail!"

"Just relax; lay back and keep your mouth shut. I'll have you out of here in a few days," Thomas Bena shrugged.

"You are going to have to take care of things at the casino. My top two lieutenants are out of the picture now and I don't want the casino falling apart," Joey said.

"Do you want me to get Vinny back here?"

"No, the place will really go to hell."

"Who can take the reins then?"

"Just have the department managers take care of their sections and you oversee everything and report back to me, daily."

"Yeah, I think I can swing that."

"Okay, I'm puttin' a lot of faith into you, Thomas only because you did some good work for my father. Don't disappoint me," Joey said.

Thomas stood up with a nod and said , "I'll be in touch Joey,"

The senior Scapalini was a ruthless man. Thomas was having a hard time adjusting to life with Joey. He wasn't convinced Joey had enough backbone to keep things in control. The elder Scapalini would have buried people left and right to clean up a mess like this.

Chapter 27

The U.S. law enforcement officers walked out the door of the airport into the humidity of Mexican air. RJ shed his jacket and slipped it through the strap of his carry-on briefcase.

Humidity for RJ felt like suffocation; having lived most of his life in the arid climate of Arizona.

Special Agent in Charge Orville Mann turned to look at his team of two agents and Detective Jones walking towards him. He had one more task to accomplish to put a tight lid on this case; and then he could focus on his retirement.

He had brought RJ, with the permission of his captain, because he spoke an intermediate level of Spanish, and because RJ held the right of first discovery on this case. Mann liked the kid as a law enforcement officer and he had decided to groom him for a spot in the bureau. If he could pull that off, he could live vicariously through RJ even after his retirement.

Romero Rodriquez stood in front of a black car outside the airport. He was a Mexican Special Forces police member. Mann had done the prep work procedures for the capture and extradition back to the United States of Vincent Scapalini. He wanted him back for the trail of both Scapalini brothers. Romero held the sign that read MANN. The agents quickly walked towards him.

Agent Mann extended his hand as he approached.

"Officer Rodriquez, I'm Agent Mann. I spoke with you on the phone."

The agents traveled light; each shouldered only a carry on bag, They placed the bags in the trunk of the vehicle. Next, the five men squeezed into the small car and were driven by Rodriguez into headquarters.

Acapulco was like an aging show girl; sagging in certain places. This effect was not uncommon in Las Vegas. Other Mexican resort towns had stolen Acapulco's thunder in the past decades. It had fallen from favor with American tourists.

The car sped through various streets and arrived at police headquarters; a white building with POLICIA written on the side in black letters. The group got out, walked into the building and immediately discovered there was no air conditioning other the spinning ceiling fans.

The American agents walked through a maze of hallways that ended in a room containing six Mexican officers dressed in black commando gear.

The commander, in a police uniform, sat at a dilapidated desk it the front of the room. Cigarette smoke hung thick in the air; circling the machismo. When the agents entered, each group of trained law enforcement men ogled the other; evaluating apparent strengths and pinpointing hidden weakness.

American law enforcement carried a certain mystique in under-developed countries; mostly created by Hollywood. But the Mexican officers reeked of machismo and felt they could meet or exceed the skills of the Americans; with Mexican street savvy if nothing else.

The meeting got underway with a description of the target. Mann handed the arrest warrant over to the Mexican officer in charge of the operation. He stuffed a half smoked cigar between his teeth to leaf through the documents; grunted his approval.

The young bucks around the room watched the goings on with practiced indifference.

"It's very important that the suspect isn't harmed," Mann said knowing that these kids, like all green officers, could get itchy trigger fingers and have a lower level of respect concerning suspects rights; especially once the adrenaline started flowing. He looked at RJ and said, "Can you tell them that?"

"Es muy importante esta hombre es no herida," RJ said haltingly

Scattered chuckles drifted around the room. RJ wasn't sure if he had said a word incorrectly, or it the concept of no harm made them chuckle.

Mann looked at RJ with concern but knew that he had to incorporate the Mexican team in order to stay within international laws. The thought had occurred to him to get them to unload their weapons going in; but he knew they would never go along with that plan. And neither would he if the tables had been turned.

"Tell them we must be very careful because this guy is a very dangerous criminal," Mann spoke to RJ.

"Nesicitamos muy cuidad porque esta muchacho es muy peligro."

"After the briefing, the American agents began to suit up with Kevlar vests and collected and re-checked weapons they had turned over at the airport. Upon arrival they had been returned. Even though they weren't going to lead the raid, Mann wanted his team safe.

It was almost noon and Mann was anxious to get going. Vinny's habit of partying late and sleeping late meant the current time of the day would be perfect for the element of surprise.

The group jumped back into the tiny car and Rodriquez followed the black van containing the Mexican police through the busy streets of Acapulco. The van stopped at a villa squeezed in between a hotel and some other apartments. The men poured out of the vehicles and ran up the stairs to a third floor condo. They stopped to assemble outside the door of the condo.

On cue, two of the Mexican cops swung a heavy steel battering ram against the door close to the locking mechanism. The door crashed open back into the room as the remaining cops flooded into the apartment.

"Policia, no mueve," They roared, over and over.

The FBI agents remained outside the door jam; guns drawn and waiting, but were shocked when the shooting started.

Mann and the other agents rushed in behind the Mexican team; darting carefully to avoid the line of fire. At that moment, the shooting ceased. Smoke from the guns drifted slowly through the air; the stench of gunpowder burned Mann's eyes. After blinking numerous times, he saw three men lying on the living room floor of the condo.

One of the wounded was a Mexican cop, but the other two were Caucasian men; one wasn't moving. RJ saw a wound on his head. The other, lay moaning on the on the floor. He cringed as his pant leg darkened; slowly absorbing the blood that oozed from a leg wound.

A Mexican officer held a submachine gun inches from his head and screamed, "No mueve! No mueve!"

RJ not knowing the exact words he needed to control the shooting; shouted "No mas! No mas!" And then realizing there were english speaking people in the room, shouted "Everybody freeze, cease fire!

Several tense seconds passed as everyone standing held their guns pointed down but watching like wound springs.

"No mas,' RJ said with a lowered voice and the guns followed as adrenaline ebbed. His knees trembled with relief as the guns found their way back to holsters. "No mas," he whispered to himself.

The rest of the condo was cleared by team effort. Mann walked over to the two Caucasian men and held a photo of Vinny Scapalini next to their faces. Neither white face matched the photo; Mann felt the hair on the back of his head stand. A combination of anger and concern boiled inside of him.

His fears; that they had hit the wrong condo, and his second one that they had a dead guy to explain, added to the concern, as well as a wounded cop. How would he explain all this to the judge who had written the warrant?

The wounded police officer was hauled to the hospital and the other wounded person was cuffed and taken to the hospital also. Before he left, with one of the FBI agents assigned to escort him until they could run his prints, Mann questioned him.

"Where is Vinny Scapalini?" Mann asked.

"Is that what this is all about?" the body guard asked.

"Just answer my question," Mann returned.

"I don't know where he is," the guard said, grimacing.

"Aren't you supposed to be protecting him?"

"He wanted to go south to a party last night; we lost track of him at the party."

"Where was the party?"

"San Marcos. Now can I go to the hospital before I bleed to death?"

Mann nodded to the cops and they took him out of the condo on a backboard. He turned to RJ and said, "I knew those trigger happy bastards were going to screw this up."

"Yeah," RJ agreed, putting his gun back into his holster. "Now things are going to get even more complicated."

"Maybe not," Mann said, "We just have to drop these cowboy's and go solo."

The element of surprise may have been lost so Mann left two agents at the scene and departed to plan their next strategy, without the troops. Unfortunately, they would have to go down to San Marcos tonight, if they planned to catch Vinny unawares and lurking in his element. The team reassembled, they rented two cars and headed an hour south into a sleepy fishing village. The town tried hard to cash in on the gold flowing from Acapulco. Several bars and clubs had sprung up along the costal shoreline and Agent Mann decided to split the team up to make the search quicker.

Sure that every team member was on the same radio frequency he sent two agents south and dropped RJ off at a club in town, then drove himself to a bar just outside of town.

RJ, now dressed in a more casual shirt that he had picked up in a shop in Acapulco, did his best to look the part of an American tourist. The neon sign over the club door blinked El Mar. He walked into the dark beneath the blinking sign and took a good long look around. The patrons were a varied group that consisted of about seventy five percent American tourists; wealthy ex-patriots traveling the Mexican coast.

RJ pulled a stool up to the bar, and then ordered a rum and coke. He sat there nursing the drink so he could gaze surreptitiously in the mirror behind the bar. The faces of people at the tables scattered throughout the club were clearly visible from that vantage point.

Fifteen minutes later, RJ figured he had struck out but decided at the last minute to show Vinny's photo to the bartender. He reached in his pocket to withdrawal the photo and heard commotion from around the corner. He froze; then listened for a moment.

"No, get back here you bitch," a gruff voice shouted back.

RJ heard the unmistakable New York accent roar across the room. A sign read 'Banos' with an arrow after it; as if pointing in the direction of the scuffle. He stood and walked quickly around the corner of the bar; then stood face to face with Vinny Scapalini. The very large man had a tight grip around the wrist of a screaming Mexican prostitute. As she struggled to get away Vinny twisted her arm again and looked up at the intruder.

"What are you looking at you little punk?" Vinny said with his trademark spittle flying. RJ responded by raising his hands slighty and saying, "I'm just trying to use the bathroom."

"Well can't you see it's busy?"

"Help me, Senior!" the prostitute pleaded.

"Shut up, bitch," Vinny said.

Then turned back to RJ and said, "Go piss outside."

RJ saw the bartender starting to react; and then realized he would have to do something. He didn't want the Vinny apprehension attempt to fail again.

He grabbed Vinny's free hand and than planted a punch on his nose. The blow landed on a crooked spot which indicated it may have been broken before. The punch served to launch Vinny out of his alcoholic stupor.

He howled his rage immediately. Then released his grip on the prostitute and reached back and down into his waistband for his gun. RJ saw it coming and gripped the gun as it appeared.

He threw all his weight into the two hundred plus pound bulk of enraged Italian; to throw his off balance. Vinny stumbled back into a fall that reduced a table to kindling.

RJ jumped right in and pinned Vinny to the pile of rubble. Next RJ heard the distinct click of a gun being clicked behind his ear. He twisted around slowly to see the twin barrels of a side by side sawed off shotgun inches away from his face.

The bartender growled, "Don't move. Somebody call La Policia."

Behind him the patrons of the club formed a semi-circle; the rest of the patrons made a hasty retreat.

RJ stood slowly; hesitant to release his hold on Vinny's weapon. He didn't know if Vinny had friends here and he wasn't going to make his identity known to anyone. Instead he leaned against the corner of a wall; clandestinely the mike of a small radio they all carried; was keyed. At the same time he started speaking Spanish to the bartender; assuming Vinny wouldn't be able to understand what was said.

RJ told the bartender, Vinny had caused the problem and damages; but that he would be willing to cover the cost of the damaged furniture.

The bartender motioned towards the door with the shotgun and said "Sale," which meant "Leave" in Spanish. Fully expecting a gun battle to begin; RJ moved his hand down towards the gun under his shirt slowly and simultaneously released his grip on Vinny's gun. But to his surprise, Vinny's eyes focused on something behind RJ; the blood drained from Vinny's face.

RJ looked out of the corner of his eye to see three FBI agents, standing behind him; guns drawn and trained on Vinny Scapalini.

Vinny recognized Agent Mann; his gun slipped out of his hand. He melted in a heap on the floor.

"Hi Vinny, funny meeting you here," Agent Mann said, then putting his hand on RJ's shoulder said," I see you've met my friend."

Vinny was silent as they led him away in cuffs. Agent Mann busily produced documents to the bartender; explaining why American federal agents were in his club arresting people. The agents eased out of the club with Vinny in tow and then made a hasty retreat back to the hotel room in Acapulco.

The next day Agent Mann made various phone calls to arrange the transfer of the dead body guard body back to the U.S. The other bodyguard couldn't be immediately moved so one of the agents would stay in Mexico to accompany him back in a few days.

The rest of them made their way to the airport; boarded a plane and sat in the last row of the aircraft. Vinny got planted in the middle seat; with an agent on each side of him. On the short trip home, he vacillated between sleeping off his hangover and whining about his headache. When he slept the snore was obnoxious and his head drifted on occasion over to Agent Mann's shoulder; and was immediately pushed away. The three hour flight back to Las Vegas was uneventful and the group exited the plane last; and then walked down the stairs on the exterior of the passenger walkway.

Two black cars parked at the bottom of the stairs and discharged two more men. The FBI agents drove the returning group back to FBI headquarters.

CHAPTER 28

The next morning Vinny awoke in the Clark County Jail. Transported from FBI headquarters in Las Vegas the night before, but Vinny refused to cooperate; except to demand medical care for his fractured nose and to ask for his attorney. The scene at the FBI building found Agent Mann in the jail hoping it would loosen up his tongue. The jail cell only encouraged the despicable behavior. The results placed him on a morning ride to a crowded emergency department. Three hours of overworked doctors, nurses, X-ray techs ended with Vinny still wailing all the way to the jail and into the next night. Predawn increased the throbbing in Vinny's head to non-stop tremors; the prison physician decided to deliver Vinny into Valium and Demerol heaven.

Late afternoon found VInny placing a call to Thomas Bena with a plea for representation. Hours passed. The arrival of the mafia family's attorney stalled the momentum and the interrogation room was filled with all the important people; Agent Mann, a federal prosecutor, Thomas Bena and Vinny. The FBI room filled with high powered players each with their own personal stake ; a high level chess game with the corresponding high priced consequences.

In spite of Vinny's near constant alcoholic haze, he could be a nasty foe when cornered and now the haze had somewhat cleared during his containment. He reverted back to anticipating his enemy's moves like a veteran chess player.

Thomas Bena detested Vinny's drunken binges; he had to admit Vinny approached problem solving much like his father's generation of the mob; when gangsters ran New York City. That now gone, group of power players withered the foe that stood in their white hot glare. Brother Joey spent too much time negotiating; too much time playing kiss ass to maintain control.

When Vinny called, Thomas began to position himself such that this whole situation would benefit him as a future power broker; beyond his usual monetary fee's. Thomas had just come from Joey's prison visit. The FBI had played that chess move well. Joey could spend years in prison. Back at FBI headquarters with Vinny, Thomas was tiring of the game.

Two agents brought Vinny in wearing his XXL neon orange jumpsuit. His nose visibly swollen; his eyes in the raccoon stage of bruising. Thomas Bena immediately began voicing objections of police brutality upon seeing Vinny's face; secretly, he figured Vinny deserved it, but he wanted to put the Feds on the defensive right at the start.

"Mr. Bena, your client got into a fight in Mexico. We just happened to show up, probably kept him from getting killed," Mann responded to Bena's complaints.

"That's bullshit," Vinny shot back, "that guy was one of yours."

"Not true, Mr. Scapalini, the guy with whom you were in an altercation with is not employed by the FBI," Mann said.

"Bullshit," Vinny said.

"Your choice of a fighting opponent is not the issue here, Mr. Scapalini," Mann said.
"We had and still have an international arrest warrant for you, and here you are," Mann looked straight at Vinny. "Now maybe we can move on."

Dried, crusty blood rimmed Vinny's nostrils; puffy red streaked eyes glared at the agents across the table.

"Exactly what is the charge against my client?" Thomas Bena interjected.

"The murder of Joseph Rains."

Vinny's eyes looked away. His gaze drifted around the room. No apparent physical reaction upon hearing the charge against him. Inside, his heart thumped thick blood as his mind raced; searching for possible ways to get out of this bind. Jack would have been the perfect scapegoat, but he knew forensics would show the evidence wouldn't hold that up. Thomas Bena read Vinny's thoughts and calculated accordingly; like a wolf testing the air, he lowered his head in wait for the next sign.

Cogitating this whole scenario on his leisurely drive to Vinny's rescue; the next clue on the wind would lead him into the kill; the one that would deliver the casino into his hands, free and clear of the Scapalini family.

The time spent caring for the casino, under Joey's request has spawned a number of schemes. Thomas knew that with Joey out of the picture he could control the entire situation with much greater ease. Here stood Vinny in the jaws of steel, waiting for Thomas to spring him. The lawyer's mind whirled like a well oiled machine.

Vinny in charge of the casino would be an ace in the hole. He would either be drunk all the time or unavailable allowing Thomas private time to manipulate the casino business to his advantage. He knew that most of the Scapalini fortune had been obtained illegally; he wanted a large portion. Vinny could meet his demise through alcoholism or violence at any time. And he was so easy to lead.

"Bena! Do you have some advice for your client?"Agent Mann raised his voice and took control of the silence.

Thomas snapped back to focus on the situation at hand. Power in his veins; he was completely at ease in this environment. FBI agents and prosecutors continued to be major players in his life game. He understood their rules well. Prior to this conference, he and Vinny had agreed as to what deal they might offer the Feds. Bena took a deep breath; fine tuning his negotiation skills before he spoke; this group of sharks could taste blood and were ready to move in for the kill.

"My client has information that could benefit your case."

"I'm all ears," Mann said.

Vinny still in a sour mood, cleared his throat and in a raspy voice said, "I witnessed the murder of that Mormon guy."

"Who would that be?" Agent Mann asked, forcing Vinny to reveal more; hoping he would stumble out another clue to what actually happened.

"The guy you just said," Vinny replied.

"He's referring to Joseph Rains," Thomas Bena piped up.

"How did you witness this?" Mann asked.

Vinny looked at Thomas Bena and did not answer the question. Thomas Bena unfolded his hands.

"Before we get into the details, we want to talk about what my client will get out of this."

"Isn't that funny it's all about you!" Mann sneered, "We can help you, if you help us. There's not much we can deal with, until we know what you have to offer."

"How about motive, method and prime suspect," Bena said.

"Sounds interesting, but is it supposition or do you have proof?"

"The evidence is there and you have it all there in front of you," Bena growled.

"And what your terms or should I say demands?"

"We want complete immunity from prosecution for my client," Bena said.

Agent Mann started the laughter. which roared around the room. "I tell you what, give us some time to discuss this," Mann said as he and his team left the room. RJ and some others had been left to watch the suspect and his counsel, from the viewing window.

Thomas Bena wasn't sure if they had taken the bait or not and to release the tension he made small talk with Vinny.

"It looks like the bear is about to eat it's own," the prosecutor said.

"Yeah I think he's going to turn states witness on his brother," Mann said.

"There's no way we can give him complete immunity," the prosecutor said.

"If we can bring Joey down, this family will cease to be a thorn in the bureau's ass," Mann said.

"Let's at least put up a good front and maybe he will take a fifteen to twenty stint," the prosecutor returned.

"Agreed," Mann said and led the procession back into the room.

The negotiations continued on for another two hours and in the end Vinny got complete immunity. Mann hated to think about this scum bag walking the streets, but everyone knew Vinny was a self destructive bomb just waiting to go off. He would eliminate himself soon enough.

Agent Mann could now end his career with a big Mafia fish and the world would be better off for it.

RJ had been a fly on the wall through this whole drama. His interest heightened each day. He thought he might do okay with these head games and decided to take up the idea of him moving over to the FBI side of things when he returned to Flagstaff.

Thomas Bena was on top of the world; life was good when legal wrangling came his way.

Vinny couldn't get the smirk off his face, even with the pain from his nose and a hangover that just wouldn't quit. He had dumped the goods on Joey without a second thought.

The Feds taped him telling the story. Joey had killed Rake Rains in a fit of rage, because the old man had refused the third purchase offer on Bruja Canyon.

Jack had gone back up there to dispose of Rake's body. Joey's gun was found at the scene of the crime and bullets from that gun had killed Rake and his dog. Other witnesses had been found; like the gas station attendant who placed Joey in St. George on the day of the murder in the black Hummer. Chiara's car was located in the casino; Michael would testify that he was told to bury it. Life looked glum at best for Joey.

Thomas Bena left the headquarters with Vinny by his side. He immediately called Joey in prison to resign as his defense attorney. He told him he didn't have faith in the case.

Joey smelled a rat but he had to beat this rap before he could figure this out; meanwhile a cloud formed around him.

CHAPTER 29

The wedding plans progressed at an acceptable pace, only two months after the Bruja Canyon incident. Chiara and Jason agreed a quick wedding would be best; considering the traumatic events surrounding that time.

Jason and Chiara had been sucked down into that hole of doubt and fear of the future. Jason's sense of immortality and dissipated with the trauma of Chiara's accident and the resulting aftermath.

Chiara continued to ride the roller coaster of emotional changes. She was up most days but on occasion fell back toward the pit of despair.

Jason wrote it off as post traumatic stress disorder, but one episode in particular alarmed him. Chiara's blue mood had deteriorated to the point of wedding cancellation. For the week following; Chiara refused to talk about it or much else. It only ended after Jason, contacted her mother. Connie called Chiara and asked her to come to L.A. and spent some time with her.

"Hello Mother," Chiara said after Connie opened the door of her apartment.

"Come in Dear," Connie said, hugging her daughter tightly.

They walked into her living room and sat down. Connie brought water for both of them. A bit of small talk followed.

"Okay Mom what's the urgent need for me to drive over here?" Chiara asked.

She never enjoyed her trips to Los Angeles; spending a significant amount of time in outdoor settings, Chiara found the squalor and violence agitating.

Connie insisted on living in the barrio. she felt it kept her closer to her roots. When Chiara was in the city she couldn't wait to be driving out and had a hard time relaxing until that time.

"Jason called, pretty distraught," Connie started, "You called off the wedding?"

"I just get down and I'm not sure Jason can understand. He's the kind of person who's always upbeat and I think I need to marry someone who can relate to how I'm feeling," Chiara said.

"When you start to have those feelings, the last thing you need is to be around someone who is also sad," Connie said.

Chiara sat with a frown on her face and a vacant gaze in her eyes as if she was many miles away.

"There's something I've never told you. Now that you are getting over that crisis you experienced and are about to wed you need to know," Connie continued. A lump formed in her throat.

"I met your father when I was a young girl living in Spain. We were lovers, and I got pregnant. The problem was my father was very strict and I was afraid of what he would do, so I left home. Your father's name was Ernesto. He was from the states and had family here; but I couldn't live with him, because he travelled a lot," Connie said.

Chiara was suddenly attentive, "What year was that?" she asked.

"You were born in 1961, so that was 1960," Connie replied.

"What was my father's last name?" Chiara asked, visibly working on a concept.

"I know it's going to sound strange but, I only spent a couple nights with him and never learned his last name, so I gave you my last name."

"What happened next?"

"He returned to the United States and he sent enough money to fly me to America, which is where you were born."

"Why are you telling me this now?" Chiara asked.

"Because, your father committed suicide shortly after he returned to the states, it's the part of his medical history that you need to know because you seem to be displaying similar symptoms. I am very concerned about you."

"Why did you wait so long to tell me this?"

"At first, I was ashamed. So I invented a story that he had died in a car crash," Connie said, "then I hoped that his psychological problems may have skipped a generation."

Chiara just sat and shook her head, trying to absorb the news of her father and his mental health issues and subsequent suicide.

Connie went into the kitchen to fix sandwiches. Chiara needed time to think.

Finally, she looked up and said," So you think the problems I'm having with Jason are something I inherited from my father?"

"No I'm not saying that the problems you are having in your relationship may be due to this or something else entirely, but you have to consider all the possibilities."

"So where do I go with this? I love Jason and I want this to work out," Chiara said.

"Jason knows what I've just told you. I talked to him when you were missing," Connie replied, "but after you were found , with all the excitement and media attention, I couldn't find time to get you alone to discuss this."

"So that's why he's been acting so strange recently."

"Jason is really good for you and vice a versa, but I think you need to seek out professional help, as well." Connie said.

"A shrink?"

"In this day and age, a therapist is very fashionable; at least in this city."

"But I live in a different culture, one that doesn't really fancy all that chic clective psychotherapy stuff," Chiara said.

"It may be the difference between life and death," Connie said, becoming more insistent. "You've seen the signs yourself."

"Okay, Mother," Chiara said rolling her eye's.

"Chiara, you are my only child, if you won't do it for yourself, then do it for me."

After a night of tossing and turning, her mind was squirming like a bag of snakes; Chiara left L.A. the next morning. The visit with her mother launched the subconscious voice in side her head into endless questioning and speculation about her past. The drive gave her space, privacy and time to embrace this new knowledge of who she might be. She made one stop to fill her gas tank on the trip home. Then she drove straight through to Littlefield, in a trance-like state.

The house was dark when she pulled into the gravel lot, but Isa whined and barked at the sound of the car on the gravel. Chiara's body, stiff from the drive, needed a stretch. When she walked through the door, Isa mobbed her; tail wagging with obvious affection and delight. Chiara hunkered down to rub and scratch the dog.

She wished the endless optimism dogs seemed to possess would come and live inside her. She walked to the couch and plopped down. Steg sauntered with his king of the house swagger out of the bedroom. The purr and leap up on her lap demanded affection. The sound of crunching gravel outside brought her to her feet. She watched Jason's vehicle pull into the drive. When he saw her car, he came running for the door; a moment later Jason enveloped her in his arms.

"I missed you! I am so glad you made it home safe and sound. How is your Mom?" his words breathless and warm on her neck.

"Ok. She's okay," Her voice flat and sounding tired. It felt good to have Jason's arms around her; the long drive of the trip and the new knowledge she had carried home weighed her down.

Jason so filled with good news, failed to judge her blue mood.

"Hey, I landed a carpentry job and will start in a week! Building houses outside of Vegas. That'll help with the bills considerably!" the words tumbled from him. He reached for Chiara again; the air seemed to chill around her, "What about you? How are you? You seem, well, not okay," he stepped back to look at her face and into her eyes. "What is it Chiara? What? Tell me."

"I did a lot of thinking on the drive home," Chiara said, "Mom told me what you already knew about my father. I am still not sure how I feel about all that right now. But it does explain a lot of things."

Several hours later the conversation ended with Jason and Chiara more committed than ever. Both agreed to honestly communicate everyday. They celebrated the new job with pizza and candles and the next day Chiara made an appointment with a therapist in Mesquite.

Chiara wanted to resume her desert running, but found it difficult. Fear followed in her; memories of falling into Bruja Canyon made her cautious every time she went out. She realized the fear was her own creation and she was determined to overcome it. The idea to shorten

Ken England   193

her runs and train within areas that were within sight of the house was a good start.

In addition, Jason insisted she take a vow to always let him know where she was going and never change that plan. Each time she felt less fear and was very thankful that Isa chose to be her constant running partner.

During the next week Chiara had her first visit with a therapist. The event was long and difficult and immediately turned into a soul bearing session. It left her emotionally angry and the therapist encouraged her to use the running as a way to dissipate the unwanted emotions. She left the therapist's office and searched a way to shake loose the despair. The short runs around the house wouldn't accomplish this. She decided on the way home to take a longer run.

She changed into her running clothes and shoes and jotted out a quick note for Jason. Then collected Isa into her yellow Subaru just back from the FBI crime lab and headed out to the desert for her first good long run.

CHAPTER 30

The veteran attorney was used to baby sitting these gangsters but after three days decided that it was time that Vinny stood up to the plate and took the lead. Two days of work later, he finally looked presentable in public.

Vinny walked through the doors of the Crown Jewels Casino. The swagger befitted the King of the Castle. Boiling under that swagger was anger that etched his face and still puffed his eyes; dark eyes exhibiting the first signs of jaundice, the possibility of early liver failure. Employees, and the public, wondered, whispers hissed to follow him after passing each group in the casino. In the surveillance room, Stevie picked him up and tracked his progress with several ceiling cameras.

"Here comes trouble," he said to the other technician in the room. A sentiment shared by everyone under the casino roof.

Vinny walked into Joey's office. When he was about to pass Vanessa's desk, he stopped and stood glaring at her behind the desk. His eyes dropped to her ample breasts.

"I'll have them," he thought to himself."

He snarled at her, "Get me some coffee," and then walked into the office.

Vanessa quickly called room service. When it arrived she had them deliver it to him themselves. The last thing that she wanted to do was be alone with Vinny, because she was extremely uncomfortable.

She breathed a huge sigh of relief when Thomas Bena arrived to announce he had plans to keep Vinny occupied for most of the day. When the attorney walked into the office, he found Vinny stretched out on Joey's Victorian couch.

Partly because he was tired and partly as a way a defying Joey's authority; Vinny had never been able to relax in this office until now.

He lay there imagining Joey, sleeping on a steel cot in prison, hoping they would be the worst nights of his brother's life. During his stroll through the casino Vinny was conjuring up a list of people that he would fire; most of them were Joey's henchmen.

But Thomas Bena put the brakes on that notion; arguing that they had to keep the peace around the casino. If he started indiscriminately firing people; the employees would fight back with bad attitudes and poor customer service. All that would mean less income for the casino. A domino effect would eventually result in a loss of revenue or worse.

When Joey got the resignation call from Thomas Bena, his attorney; he knew the gig was up. Something big went down and he wasn't a part of it. Immediately he phoned another attorney he had known from the old neighborhood. Smelling the bloom of money from the desert; the legal representative put a hold on all other cases and flew to Mesquite the next day.

He met with Joey for three hours in the prison, then the first move he made was to pressure the judge to set bail. The prosecutor in the case worried any more delays might risk the loss of the entire case.

A call to Vanessa indicated the current state of affairs at the casino to be dismal. She took the call at her desk just outside Joey's office. Joey sensed her tension and her danger and told her to go down to the casino and find another phone then call him back.

Vanessa cognizant of her role with Joey understood, even though she had fallen in love with him, the only label he would have for her in the future was mistress. Still she loved him and would do anything for him even if it involved some danger. She left her desk in search of another phone to call Joey. They spoke for five minutes and he gave her a list of exactly what he needed and how to go about it. The plans made her a little uncomfortable but she knew she had to pull this off.

As she walked through the main lobby the hotel operator paged her name on the overhead speakers. She picked up the nearest courtesy phone and was informed she was requested back at her desk immediately.

She entered hesitantly. Vinny leaned back in Joey's office chair, his feet parked on the mahogany desk. Her mind flashed back to the many nights she had lain on that desk with Joey.

"Where the hell have you been?" Vinny barked.

"I had to use the restroom," she replied.

"Get in here I want you to type a letter."

"Yes sir," she said timidly.

"And close that damn door!"

Vanessa closed the door, walked into the office and sat in front of the desk facing Vinny with a pad in her hand; her eyes on the paper.

"No one seems to understand, that now I'm running the show here. Joey isn't coming back."

"What exactly do you want me to write?" Vanessa asked, trying to remember the shorthand she had learned many years ago.

"I want to send a memo to all the managers in this place," he said.

"Go ahead," she said.

"Have each manager schedule a meeting with me," Vinny said.

He was the boss now and he should have everything his brother had, Vinny told himself; then turned his head to look at Vanessa up and down, as she jotted the few notes down.

He stood, stretched, growled with pleasure and began a strut around the desk. He stopped to pick up a sword that leaned against the corner of the desk. In one slow motion he unsheathed the gleaming blade and moved it above his head, slicing the air with a swishing sound; back and forth. A drop of drool slipped down from the corner of his mouth.

"Have you ever seen my brother's sword collection?" Vinny asked.

"Uh, no," Vanessa stammered, eyes watching the steel move through the air.

"Swords are for wimps," he sliced again. "I like guns; something with more punch. But this blade is about as sharp as they come, you could probably take a person's head off with this thing."

Vanessa swallowed hard. Vinny lowered the sword and placed it against her throat. Grinning, his eyes squinted closed; more spittle slipped out of his mouth.

The deformed nose dropped dramatically down, to plow a grotesque path toward Vanessa. The snout stopped four inches in front of her eyes. The image of the pocked and purple alcohol saturated bulb coming at her gagged fear in her throat and made her pulse pound. Vinny pressed the blade between her skin and the silk tank top she wore.

With a quick twist of his wrist the Samurai sword cut through her top and the straps of her bra; full breasts swelled with absolute exposure. They rose, then fell back with rapid respirations of fear. She clinched her eyes afraid to see what might come next.

The sight of the heaving pearl white breasts snapped Vinny from the venomous mood; he understood why his brother had hired her to sit out at the desk in front of his office.

"Everybody knows you aren't a receptionist, you're just a whore for my brother," Vinny hissed

Vanessa smelled the stench of him even before she opened her eyes to see his face closer now. Nail polish remover breath reeked from him. In one rushing move Vinny grabbed her arms, lifted her up to a standing position then spun her around toward the desk.

"I figure anything that was his is now mine."

No words came; only thoughts of what she could do to save her life. Vinny swept an arm across the desk. Joey's personal items exploded onto the floor in one swipe. Vinny pushed Vanessa down until her back came to a stop on the polished mahogany.

"This is a familiar place for you, huh?" Vinny sneered.

He laid blade against her thigh, and then slipped it up inside the seam of her skirt.

Next he gave a quick twist; material popped and exploded like a parachute off the desktop. Vinny fumbled with his pants; searching for lost manhood.

Vanessa was no prude and had even done a brief stint as a call girl but this violence and vulnerability rolled stomach bile into her throat. It took everything she had to reach down into her gut and steel herself enough to speak.

"There's something you need to know," she said.

"I have everything I need right here."

"Vinny, I really like you and I could see us spending a lot of time together, but Joey has kept some secrets from you. I found one out in an intimate moment," her voice low and suggestive, in an attempt to stop the coming rape.

Vinny paused then said, "That can wait."

He lowered himself upon her. The weight of his gut pushed against her belly.

"They are stealing what is rightfully yours, right now!"
she said in his ear; desperation in her voice, "Vinny, I'll be right here waiting for you, but you have to hurry or there won't be anything left!"

Vinny stopped and with a queer look in his eye lifted himself up, and then leaned back in to raise his hand as if to slap her across the face.

She winced at the sight of the square sweaty palm inches above her head; the blow never came. He hiked up his trousers and staggered toward the door.

"Stupid bitch, talks too much."

Suddenly he spun around, came back and grabbed her by the throat, "If you're lyin', I'm goin' to kill you!" he snarled.

Vanessa stared silently at the side of his face; praying, waiting, hoping he would take the bait. Then she remembered another detail Jocy had shared with her in one of their moments. However she had never seen the alleged booty.

She described a bunker that Joey had built in the desert. Riches inside included; gold bars, jewelry' and a literal ton of cash. This, of course, was straight out of Vanessa's imagination. She gave Vinny directions to a place she had overheard Michael talking about. And told Vinny that Joey had contacted some of his still loyal security guards to go and clean it out. Vinny took the directions and stormed out of the door.

She sat there quivering with immediate relief at the thought of what could have happened. Completely naked; she snatched the sword and wrapped the split skirt around it . She walked to Joey's closet, choose a dress shirt, jacket and a pair of slacks, slipped them on and left. She pressed the sword against her body and moved swiftly out of the office.Then she moved swiftly down the service elevator and out through the garage.

CHAPTER 31

Chiara stopped her car on a dirt road halfway to Mesquite. The area looked completely innocuous, if not a bit boring, but it was the kind of area that would fit well into Chiara's comfort level.

The desert stretched endlessly before her; punctuated with Ocotillo bushes and yuccas of all types and sizes. Isa whined anxiously. She scurried back and forth in the back seat; excited to run even before they had left the house.

Chiara opened the yellow car door. Isa jumped out and then bounced in place waiting for the go signal. Her muscles were tight springs; she wouldn't leave Chiara's side but clearly stated her impatience.

"Easy, girl friend. I don't warm up as fast as you.."

Chiara stretched and strapped the water bottle around her waist; she needed this run as bad as Isa.

After the bombshell her mother had dropped on her about her father's suicide and the resulting session with the therapist; she began to imagine what it would feel like to let go of the past and release the built up tension of the present.

The physical exertion of running went a long way toward relaxing her on the deepest echelon. It was her form of meditation.

On a level road like this one, Chiara could run back-to-back six minute miles for much of the day.

"Let's go!"

Isa leapt with joy and immediately bounded off to follow a multitude of desert scent trails. The dog covered three times the distance that the human could cover. She had to call Isa back from time to time as she ranged further and further in the canine hunter zigzag course.

Nellis Federal Penitentiary, austere even at a distance intimidated Vanessa; the thought of being locked inside with the criminals was horrifying.

The gray concrete building was surrounded by several layers of chain link fence topped with razor wire, with more razor wire sandwiched between. Guard towers punctuated the property at key locations and the modern facility was covered with dark glass much like air traffic control towers.

As Vanessa pulled into the parking lot, she wondered how any convict, much less Joey could ever walk out of the place, once captured. A cold-blooded quality surrounded the building; it seemed impossible that human life could exist inside the compound.

In the ten minutes that Vanessa waited, several guards entered the complex; through a chain link tunnel entry. All of the guards eyed the blonde suspiciously as she sat in the black sedan, waiting for Joey.

He appeared at the end of the tunnel wearing his Armani suit, paper bag in hand. The Atlantic City attorney accompanied him. The uniformed guard escorted them to a security lock space that had been walled off at the end of the tunnel. As one chain gate closed the guard radioed the tower to have the far one opened. A loud obnoxious buzzer cracked the air and the tower guard swung the gate open. The suited pair exited into the parking area and freedom.

They walked to another vehicle, stood in front of it for a few minutes and talked. Joey spotted Vanessa in his car.

Joey arrived at the black sedan; Vanessa could see he was visibly irritated. No surprise considering the events of recent days. He climbed into the passenger seat.

"Hi sweetie, I've missed you," she said and leaned over to plant a kiss on him.

Joey returned a half hearted peck and said, "We've got a lot to do honey." Thoughts of conspiracy consumed him. Unsure of the source, he didn't trust anyone at this point. Vanessa recovered without revealing how she felt about the brush off. She knew when Joey was all business to stay out of his way, "I brought the things you wanted," she said.

"Good, did Vinny take the bait?"

"Yeah, but he's really mad because he thinks you're pulling a fast one on him," she said.

"Good. The madder he is, the less clearheaded he'll be," Joey said.

"I'm afraid of what he might do to you," she said. Joey watched her face for any sign of deception.

"I can handle Vinny. I've been beating him up since we were kids," Joey said, then looking around the car asked, "Where's my gun?"

"I couldn't get a gun. Vinny's got them all locked up."

"Well then, what the hell am I supposed to do? Head butt him?"

Vanessa's face mottled, "All I could get was a sword."

Joey grew silent, then climbed into the back seat of the car, unwrapped the sword and inspected the blade. Years ago he had taken Kendo classes and learned the basics of swordsmanship.

A Samurai blade is a fascinating piece of workmanship. The ultimate sword, with the elegant arch of steel reminiscent of a few women he had known; fragile, yet deadly at the same time. Layered with soft steel in the center to maintain flexibility and covered on the outside with hardened steel to maintain that razor edge; a perfect dichotomy of delicate sophistication and lethal weapon. Perfect balance required many years to master sword maker craftsmanship.

Back in Atlantic City a rumor started that Joey had killed a competitor with this sword. Of course, like many aspects of the mystique that had developed around gangsters, this one was mostly fantasy.

Silently he put the sword down and changed into the khaki clothes that Vanessa had brought. His words broke the silence only to tell her where to make a turn; his plan would fall apart if they arrived after Vinny. Neither of them noticed the car following them from a considerable distance.

Joey instructed Vanessa to drive the car five miles down a remote dirt road, then past a large dirt pile. A half mile further they came to a large boulder. She pulled the car in behind the boulder completely concealing the car.

He ordered her to stay put and stay out of sight; then walked and jogged the distance to the pit. Ten feet deep, he reveled in the good fortune of arriving before Vinny.

Sword clutched in his right fist he walked behind the dirt pile and hunkered down, half leaning against the pile. the steel of the Samurai sword gleamed in the sun. Joey worried about a flash of light tipping his younger brother off as he approached.

"That bitch better have told me the truth," Vinny spit out under his breath. He was on his way down to the garage to get a vehicle.

"That's another thing; I drive this Hummer whenever I fuckin' feel like it," spittle flashed on to the door. Joey never allowed him to drive the vehicle when he was in charge.

Vinny opened the door and realized he didn't know where to find the keys. He spent the next two hours shouting at people until one security guard suggested he look behind the driver's side visor.

Vinny started the Hummer, roared the engine several times, and then squealed the tires out of the garage. He headed the big rig out of town, using the directions Vanessa had given him. He got lost twice; cursing her each time for his own lack of direction.

In time, he located a gravel road that had a freshly excavated pile of dirt just off the road. Exiting the road the Hummer crushed a prickly pear cactus just as Vinny saw the large hole beside his tires.

The weight of the Hummer so close to the edge of the hole the wall began to collapse enough to send loose dirt cascading down into the pit. He slammed on the brakes and cursed. Taking time to recover his heart rate from the near disaster, the realization he had missed the removal operation infuriated him to the level of near rage.

He sat inside the vehicle surveying the scene, temper boiling, saliva leaking from each side of his mouth, he uttered, "If Joey wasn't already in jail, I would kill him for this!"

There was no one around the hole and no equipment was visible. He climbed out of the vehicle. He had to see the so called bunker that Joey had constructed to hide the family riches.

A muscle cramp in Joey's right calf shouted for release. Just as the thought of standing up passed through his mind; he heard the chug of a diesel engine and the crunch of gravel.

"Vinny turning on to the road," Joey thought.

He crept to the top of the dirt pile for a peek. A half mile distant his black Hummer approached leading a small plume of dust. He slid back down the dirt pile, moved to the far end and then crouched with the sword leaning, poised and ready against his shoulder. A tremble started in the bottom of his right calf as adrenaline surged in his system and then consumed his entire body.

Vinny parked the Hummer, got out and slammed the door. He then walked between the hole and the dirt pile. He looked down eagerly into the hole searching for a door or walls, or any kind of opening that would indicate a fragment of truth to Vanessa's story. The trail between the hole and the dirt was a narrow foot and a half wide. Vinny forced his bulk close to the dirt pile and walked cautiously along it with his gun in his right hand.

Crouching at the end of the dirt pile, Joey heard the wheezing respirations coming around the heap. Vinny seconds away, had no idea his brother stood poised on the edge for bloodshed.

Joey picked up a small stone and tossed it like a hand grenade over the top of his head in a long arc. The stone just missed hitting the Hummer and bounced nosily across the hard packed desert floor. Vinny reacted immediately. He spun back around leading with his gun; ready to kill someone.

Chills ran up and down his spine. He watched for a couple seconds, but saw no one. He turned back.

The big man saw nothing, but heard a faint singing sound as the blade sliced through the air.

Something bumped his wrist. He felt no pain; merely the impact of the steel blade sharpened to surgical precision as it passed cleanly through his arm.

The quick movement startled him. He raised his right hand. Only then did he realize his hand, still gripping the gun, lay squirting arterial blood at his feet.

The realization quickly dawned on Vinny as the shock wore off that his life was in danger. He reached back to the small off his back for the 38 revolver that he kept in his waistband.

Joey lifted the sword for another blow; the fatal one. Like the bull he was, Vinny instantly reverted to primal instinct and realizing he would be too slow to stop the blade, he roared and lunged forward. He planted his large bovine head squarely into Joey's chest.

The sword swung wild. Joey fell into the dirt with two hundred and eighty pounds of Vinny on top of him.

The brother's roared, growled and rolled in a survival struggle on dry hard packed desert earth with a coating of blood on it. Vinny's severed limb spurting continuous crimson over both men. The pain in his stump was masked by endorphins; Vinny managed to retrieve the .38 from his waist and Joey clawed his brother's eyes with one hand and grabbed the gun with the other. Joey twisted the gun until he felt the bones in Vinny's fingers snap. The blood slime on the gun forced him to lose his grip on the weapon. It tumbled slow motion into the hole.

Vinny, stood with one amputated hand and broken fingers on the other; then collapsed down to his knee's. Joey's continued rage had not receded and he looked around for a weapon.

The older brother trembled above his kneeling brother to catch his breath. His eyes gazed down at the pathetic thing beside him.

"Please Joey! We're family!" Vinny cried

Joey reached for the nearby sword; receeding adrenaline ebbed his strength as he gathered to swing the blade like a baseball bat. With everything he could muster he swung a slicing blow against Vinny's throat.

The stroke not powerful to decapitate the him, passed half way through his neck; to kill him instantly.

Aortic blood sprayed a sticky liquid acknowledgement for the rightful owner of the Scapalini kingdom. Vinny's body teetered momentarily and then toppled back into the hole.

A feeling of relief and then panic washed through Joey. The rush collapsed him into the dirt. He struggled for air. The body of his only brother lay at the bottom of the hole pumping what blood was left in it, out. A flash from the blade illuminated a movement fifty feet away. A silhouetted human head and shoulders watched from a nearby rise.

CHAPTER 32

Chiara finished her run and walked into a cool down.

"Hey Isa!" she called the dog back from the small rise ahead of her. Her breaths decreased as she neared the top of the rise. Just as the dog turned back to the sound of her voice, she noticed the large black four by four parked beside a large pile of dirt and a hole.

Two men, one large and one medium sized, wrestled in the dirt. Both were covered with blood. She froze with fear; unsure of what to do next.

Even though she was an E.R. nurse she felt panicked by the violence. In slow motion the smaller man swung a shiny blade and the larger man slumped down and fell into the hole. Chiara pulled her knee's up to her chest to hide herself from the horror and to cry for what she had witnessed.

A renewed wave of panic surged through Joey as the realization settled in. Not only had he snuffed out his only sibling and was going to spend the rest of his life in confinement.

He had to bury the body and get rid of the evidence. That's when he saw Chiara.

"This can't be happening," he thought, not a witness out here in the middle of nowhere! He reached down and picked up the gun with Vinny's hand still attached.

A sharp gasp emitted from Chiara. Her stomach turned when Joey looked straight at her. Vomit heaved up her throat as he lifted the bloody hand that held a gun.

Glancing back at Chiara, Joey struggled to remove Vinny's index finger from the trigger guard.

"No witnesses! He muttered to himself ; knowing what he had to do. He and Vanessa should be planning their escape right now. Getting ready to run and leave the country so they could live the high life; for as long as they could get away with it, anyway. Only one thing stood in the way of that plan.

A distant buzzing sound reverberated in Chiara's brain and then a sudden rush of energy rushed through her body. The drama played before her in continued slow motion; like a silent dream. Unable to move; she could neither run nor utter a single noise. She collapsed as Joey fired, missing her. Joey leveled the gun again. The space between Chiara's eyebrows lined up in the sights. He prepared to put an end to this connection once and for all; to Mesquite, the casino, the Scapalini's, with a single well placed shot to an innocent girl that he didn't know.

From the top of the dirt pile the dog flashed across blue sky into a wide arch. Isa's nose had caught the familiar aroma that meant evil and pain to her. Her eye's had locked on a vision of the delivery method of that pain. Dogs don't know hatred unless they are taught how to hate. Immediate hatred riled her blood and the one human that she had bonded with and felt true love for was in danger. Joey's focus on Chiara added fuel to her fire as she dealt Joey his due. The leap covered eight feet.

Eighty pounds of well-hardened, muscled weight hit Joey like a linebacker. The impact of the dog's body knocked him sideways almost four feet and the two of them tumbled into the hole; her powerful jaws locked firmly around the human windpipe. She was in a fight to the death.

As they hit the bottom of the hole and the gun fired but Isa maintained the death grip.

Joey's throat was ripped open in the bloody vice-grip hold that two inch canines are designed to give. His trachea exposed; red frothy bubbles gurgled from the vessels. He writhed and bright red blood spurted from the gruesome tear in Joey's throat.

The body quivered in a death spasm and Isa doubled the force of her grip; instinctive and ancient predator hold delivered the final act.

At the sound of the gunshot Chiara broke down sobbing. Exhausted from the run and from the constant rush of adrenaline over the last ten minutes she dropped her head as her arms folded on her chest. Letting go, she sobbed for thirty seconds. She feared the worst had happened.

A deep shudder passed out of her lungs, followed by a long, mournful scream and then her nurse training kicked in. Standing to full height required focus and determination. The sound of nothing motivated her to run.

The sight of maimed and bloody bodies greeted her at the edge of the hole. Isa lay on her side, Chiara's voice box swelled; and then she saw a slight tail wag, but no other movement.

Chiara was afraid to jump down the hole because it was deep enough that she wouldn't be able to climb out. She searched quickly around the rim for something to help. Then she noticed the winch on the front of the Hummer. In the driver's seat she scanned for winch controls and flicking a switch she heard a high pitched whine.

With twenty feet of cable lying on the bottom of the hole, she reversed the direction of the cable and then jumped down into the hole. She drug Isa toward the cable and in response Isa lifted her blood soaked snout and licked Chiara's arm. Soothing words whispered to Isa as she feverishly worked to drag the animal.

With about ten feet of cable left in the hole, she looped the cable around Isa's body and clipped the hook back onto the cable. As the cable grew tight, Chiara stood on top off the hook and both of them slowly rose out of the hole, with Isa yipping in pain.

"It's okay baby," Chiara said. She strained to lift Isa into the backseat of the Hummer. As she lifted she felt blood coming from the dog's body. There was a bullet wound in her rib cage. Isa secure and wrapped in a blanket in the back, she jumped into the driver's seat and sped away from the scene, wiping away tears as she drove.

On a distant hillside a solitary figure in desert fatigues lowered a pair of binoculars. The close cropped gray hair was mostly hidden by a tan baseball cap. He lowered the binoculars and watched the Hummer speed away.

"That couldn't have turned out any better if I had planned it myself."

CHAPTER 33

Vanessa waited as long as she thought reasonable. She had heard the distant gunshot and then the sound of the Hummer starting. Unable to stand the suspense any longer she drove slowly up to the hole.

Complete silence crept alongside the car as it made it's way down the road. She arrived at the hole and saw the Hummer was gone. Her heart beat uncontrollably in her chest.

She got out and walked around the car until she stood at the edge to look down at the most horrifying sight she could imagine, The burn rose slowly in her esophagus as the stomach acid and the contents of her stomach began to find it's way to daylight.

Clutching her abdomen she dropped to her knees.

"What has happened?" Vanessa asked herself. Gathering her wits, she tried to get perspective on the situation. Her head spun.

"Sitting here isn't working ," she said. "It looks like a morgue down there." She couldn't even be sure which body was that of her lovers'.

Vanessa turned and hurried back to the car. She drove away; not looking back and struggling not to panic. She didn't know what to do or who to talk to. In a zombie-like state she sped back to the casino and then walked up to her desk.

When she reached for the door of Joey's office, she found it already open. Dismayed, she stood there long enough for Thomas Bena to come walking out. Noticing her numb state and chalk white face he walked over to her.

"What happened sweetheart?" he asked.

The sound of his low comforting voice lured Vanessa to step toward him, drop her head on his shoulder and begin to sob one sentence into the story, After a few choppy bits Thomas Bena took her by the arm and guided her into the office. He closed the door.

He snatched a tissue and wiped the mascara trails off her face as he told her not to repeat this story to anyone.

"Remember no one alive, knows you were out there, and you really didn't witness anything, did you?" Bena said.

"I didn't see anything," she repeated looking up at him.

Then he took her down to the garage via the service elevator and put her in his car. Next he walked over to the black sedan that Vanessa had been driving and wiped it clean of any possible prints. Then he drove her to another hotel in the area and checked her in.

"Stay here til' this whole thing blows over, Sweetheart," he said and handed her five hundred dollars cash, pulled the door shut and left.

Wailing sirens shocked Chiara out of her nightmare daze. A vigilante state trooper, who had just come on shift, stopped her for speeding on the interstate. The Hummer was so new and oddly boxed shaped that just about everybody took notice; especially when it's pushing one hundred miles per hour. she didn't see the cruiser slip in behind her.

She pulled over grudgingly, and as she came to a stop, threw the gear shift into park and jumped out, ran to the back, opened the door and crawled in with Isa.

The trooper saw the leap out of the vehicle as a threat and immediately went into combat mode. He started barking orders over the PA system and eventually stepped out with his gun drawn.

This action caused no consequence to Chiara, who was focused on Isa and had just been through her own private version of hell. Her focus was the bleeding dog that needed immediate care. Isa's eyes were open but glazed over and she didn't respond to Chiara's closeness. In her experience as an emergency nurse, Chiara knew that death more often came quietly instead of dramatically.

Another trooper arrived for back up for the first one and by then, Chiara was sure she detected no respirations in Isa. She slowly crawled out of the Hummer, covered in blood and with no concern over what the cops would do.

"Raise your hands, now lie face down," the trooper shouted through the PA. When she complied, the troopers saw the blood and a sudden urgency rose in the his voice as he continued the orders.

"Spread your arms and legs apart."

They approached the vehicle together. Then one of the troopers handcuffed Chiara as the other glanced in the side window to see the body of a dog stretched on the backseat. The pair took Chiara by her upper arms and then lifted her into a standing position.

"Did you know you were doing over a hundred miles an hour in this tank, ma'am?" the trooper asked.

"No sir," Chiara said with her head bowed, exhausted by trauma and grief of the day.

"Can you explain this?" he said gesturing to the Hummer.

"Maybe," Chiara said, dropping her head to wipe at a tear with her shoulder.

"Well?" he said, with his hands resting on his hips.

"I know this looks bad," she said, sniffing her nose, "but first there is something you need to know, there are two bodies in a hole out in the middle of the desert."

The troopers took her back to one of the patrol cars and she told the incredible story that just unfolded. Half way through, the second trooper called into his headquarters and gave directions to the bodies.

The first trooper took her into the station and she was held in an office, while they searched for a crime scene that Chiara had described.

Suddenly she was the object of extreme interest; a supervisor came into the office and questioned her intensely. A flurry of activity swirled at the station as troopers quickly came and went.

A phalanx of emergency vehicles barreled down the dirt road for over an hour to create lingering dust clouds that snaked through the desert wilderness. Two emergency vehicles collided due to the poor visibility and excessive speed, forcing incident commanders to set up a perimeter that only certain agencies were allowed through.

Outside the road block a group assembled that included state police, crime scene investigators, plus all other emergency agencies and once the word got out, a large media contingency.

The media showed up in large white trucks with satellite dishes on top. Certain specialties were allowed inside the perimeter as needed. The state police were the first to arrive, having taken the report from Chiara of a double homicide in the desert.

RJ had just left the FBI headquarters in Las Vegas, when he heard the initial calls coming over his scanner. He wasn't sure of the location of the crime scene, but it was pretty easy to follow one of the many law enforcement vehicles burning down the highway at high speeds. He arrived forty-five minutes later at a small village of emergency responders and press people outside the perimeter.

He realized he would not be able to gain access and was about to leave when one of the FBI agents that had been with him on the operation to Mexico drove by on his way out.

"Hey Jones," the other agent said, are you on this one too?"

"No I was just passing by when I heard the radio traffic."

"Well, I'm headed up to state police barracks to interview a witness. You want to tag along?"

RJ thought about for a few seconds. He had told his wife he would be home for dinner that night, but then said, "Sure, I'll follow you."

"Good, I'll fill you in up there."

RJ nodded and the two left the crime scene and drove thirty minutes to a cinder block building in a small town town just off the highway between Mesquite and Las Vegas. A painted plywood sign identified the place as the Nevada State Police Barracks. RJ and the other agent whose name was Gary huddled outside the station before going in.

"Is Mann on this one? RJ asked.

"He retired," Gary replied.

"No shit, retired?"

"Yep. just yesterday."

"I thought he was going to see this case through," RJ said.

"Well these cases can drag on for years, but this one looks like it just ended," Gary replied.

"What ya mean?"

"Didn't you hear?, both the Scapalini brothers are lying in a hole; dead as King Tut."

"You're kidding me!"

If I'm lyin', I'm dyin'! Looks like like it may be some kind of gangland style execution," Gary said.

"So who are we interviewing in here?"

"This is the real strange twist to this," the agent replied, "you remember that girl that was trapped in that canyon, north of here?"

"Chiara Martinez!?"

"One and the same."

"I worked her missing person case."

"Good I'm glad I dragged you along."

"How the hell did she get out there to witness these murders?"

"That's what we're going to find out. There's something that just doesn't smell right, huh? But either way, I think she's had a real bad year," Gary said.

The mystery of this case reached down into RJ and took hold of him once more; he was glad he had decided to come along.

The two walked into the station to conduct the interview. RJ thought Agent Mann wouldn't have wanted to miss this, but then remembered something about a sick wife, needing a lot of medical care. Still, RJ couldn't imagine being around a 'retired' Agent Mann; the guy was driven and just didn't have an off switch.

CHAPTER 34

The red pickup pulled in at the front door of the highway patrol barracks. A look of urgency and worry on his face the young man got out of his truck and walked through the front door.

Jason approached the front desk. He could feel the excitement in the air. He could also sense the presence of Chiara but it wasn't necessarily a good feeling. Her mood had changed dark again and the phone call was another shock which he had thought they were climbing out of.

The place was a small barracks; the front desk covered by a rotund woman whose responsibility was to handle both guests and radio dispatching. Presently the dispatching of state troopers occupied the majority of her time. Jason stood there unnoticed for what seemed like an hour. Soon, a uniformed trooper walked through the front door.

After exchanging the normal introductions, he walked Jason down a hallway. RJ approached from the other direction.

"Hey, Jason. How's it going?" RJ said, stopping beside Jason. Understanding the convoluted history of the entire situation, RJ took Jason aside and informed him of Isa's death and prepared him for Chiara's emotional state.

Jason walked into the office searching for Chiara. She sat on a chair in the corner. Her facial expression resembled that of a catatonic person, but when he walked over and touched her shoulder and she looked up at him and offered a timid smile. He knelt down and silently put his arms around her as best he could; the tears flowed freely in big sobs. Her shoulders shook. She rested her head in the crook of his neck and the warm tears trickled down his skin.

"I can't take this....any more....when is this going to end?" Chiara choked out.

"I don't know baby," Jason whispered, "We've dealt with the worst though. We can get through this; together we can get through anything."

They talked for another fifteen minutes. Chiara recanted the story; crying again when she told of Isa's heroic action that took the dog's life.

Before long, Gary came to the door and said that Chiara could go home with Jason.

"Unfortunately we are going to have to impound your Subaru again, until we investigate this new phase of this crime." Gary said.

Chiara nodded her acceptance in silence; she was too exhausted to respond.

"Also, I'm not sure where the other case is going to go," Gary continued, "since both of the major players are dead, there may be some indictments brought against the minor players, but I don't know right now."

"Okay," Chiara said still displaying the frown that had taken up it"s spot on her face.

"You are free to go," Gary said.

Jason and Chiara walked into the receding Nevada sunlit evening. They drove east on the interstate and dusk embraced the landscape. Car headlights on the interstate twinkled periodically. The two sat in silence, lost in their thoughts.

"I think I need a cigarette," Chiara said.

"Chiara.... you're not a smoker!" Jason said half chuckling.

"I think I might start."

"Why?"

"Why not?"

"Your health for starters."

"It doesn't seem that I'm going to live long enough to die of lung cancer," Chiara responded, looking out at the blue light over the mountains.

"You're losing it," Jason replied.

"Well think about it Jason, I'm living my life, not hurting anyone, and all of a sudden, I'm trapped in a canyon, swam a flash flood, find out my father committed suicide, got diagnosed with depression, got shot at by a madman, and lost one of my best friends."

"I swam that flash flood too, and mixed it up with that hit man.

"I know you did, that's exactly my point."

"I don't know what your point is," Jason shot back feeling exasperated and not wanting to argue right now.

"My point is, did I or you deserve any of this?'

"Nobody deserves what happened to us."

"Okay, then."

"I'm not following you."

"Okay, take that little boy diagnosed with cancer, or my father committing suicide, or all this shit that has come down on us!" Chiara said, her voice reaching a crescendo.

"It's fate, Chiara," Jason returned.

"Is it? Or is God having a bad day?"

"I've always said you get the hand dealt you. Sometimes you get four Aces, sometimes you don't."

"So that's it, my life your life everyones life is decided in one heavenly casino."

"Now that's a sight to behold."

"But think about it Jason, there is undeniably evil in this world; people doing despicable things. Like dictators or drug lords and they are doing just fine, no lightning bolts or anything. Meanwhile, the innocents of the earth suffer and get dragged to the edge of the void; some of them drop into the void. Not all of them, mind you, but something must occur on some level for these things to happen."

"It's completely random, Chiara."

"Is it? What influences or even controls people's lives, since we seemingly have no control?"

"I don't know," Jason said, turning his head away from her to roll his eyes.

"Is it God? Is it each individual, unconsciously selecting their fate? Is it some galactic crap game, or as you say, random chance?"

"Maybe it's energy waves that travel through the atmosphere and when you encounter them, your life goes haywire; like a huge wave of positive ions and boom, your life crashes or your car tire blows and you hit a tree."

"Please don't patronize me," Chiara said.

"Why is that any more far fetched than what you've been talking about?"

"I guess the real question is, do we have any control of our destiny, or is our destiny in complete control of our lives?"

"You don't think any of this is chance?"

"Let me put it in a different light, you are going to die one day, your death may seem completely logical or it may come totally out of the blue."

"And?" he said not totally wanting to know the rest.

"What I'm saying comes from the roller coaster my life has been on in this last year; and in some ways it feels like it's written out there somewhere. Maybe it's written in our genetic profile; they are finding many other things are."

"So what you are saying is that my death is programmed into my genes? Sounds like science fiction? This is wearing me out can we change the subject?" Jason asked.

"Please do," Chiara said.

As during many uncomfortable silences, Jason couldn't think of anything to talk about except the weather.

"We are supposed to have a cold front coming through tomorrow," he said.

Chiara smiled into the darkness, "Now there's a completely random topic, the weather," she chuckled softly.

Jason was greatly relieved to hear laughter after the intensity of the discussion regarding Chiara's emotional state. Another long pause ensued as they approached the lights of Mesquite.

Grandiose casino lights glittered the desert darkness. The time and temperature sign of the First National Bank of Mesquite, sat low and subdued in the flood of lights beyond it.

The temperature display sign spun on a steel post.

"Well, it's got along way to go to be considered cold," Chiara said.

"Yep, 93 degrees is definitely a long way from cold," Jason said.

RJ finished the interview with Gary and then spent time helping to write the information report. He couldn't believe how much bad luck one person could experience. It was late and RJ had missed dinner. The call home was tense and he knew that he would have to make a decision whether to stay with the state police or become an FBI agent.

The fence sitting was definitely taking a toll on his marriage. It was late for the long drive home. He didn't want to become a statistic; something he had seen many times in years as a law enforcement officer, asleep at the wheel. The best solution was to drive to Mesquite tonight and then finish up to Flagstaff in the morning.

As he swung his police cruiser off the interstate he couldn't help but notice the Crown Jewels Casino sitting among the other hotels on the mini strip there. RJ decided he would stay there, mostly out of curiosity.

Had the news affected the business or even reached here yet? He found a parking spot and carried his over night bag into the casino and then checked in at the front desk. He didn't really have the energy to hang out with all the noise and glitz and worked his way through a very crowded casino floor. The National Consortium of Shoe Sales was having it's annual convention in the hotel and the place was packed with people from all over the country.

RJ thanked his lucky stars that he had chosen law enforcement as a career and moved with some difficulty through the crowd of drunken revelers. As with all casinos, the slots and tables are on the way to everything. RJ had the elevators in sight, when something caught his attention.

An elaborately built doorway with no identification was just off the hallway to the elevators. There were two security guards standing at either side.

RJ knew that every casino, worth it's reputation, had a High Rollers Suite and he surmised this unidentified door was the entry to that particular room in the casino.

The bustle of the casino hid the news that possibly he, and he alone of all the people in the room knew; the owner's of this empire had died in a bizarre scene just hours before. Suddenly, three people walked up to the guarded entry. RJ quickly recognized the attorney that had been in the interrogation with Vinny Scapalini.

He didn't look in any way like he was grieving; he had a very shapely young woman with him and was escorting her and another individual into the suite. RJ quickly sat down at an empty slot machine that afforded him a somewhat concealed view of the subjects.

As he watched, the third person, wearing a cheap suit and somewhat disguised with an even cheaper pair of sunglasses and a khaki baseball cap turned so RJ could see his profile. RJ's jaw dropped as he strained to see the features.

The man had a keen resemblance to Agent Mann. Next a drink server walked up and asked him if he wanted a drink. He quickly turned her down, but in the time it took to say no, the trio had been swallowed up by the doors of the suite.

CHAPTER 35

Six months after the deaths of the Scapalini brothers, the Crown Jewels Casino was sold to a group of investors out of Las Vegas. Thomas Bena brokered the deal and compensation was made to the Scapalini family but the rest of the profit from the deal vaporized into an untraceable trail. Investigations into the deaths came back with no evidence of any influence form outside sources and the deaths were attributed to a family feud. The death of Rake Rains was eventually pinned on Joey due to the fact that his gun was found near the scene of the crime and it was that gun that killed Rake.

RJ sat at his desk on a beautifully sunny morning, trying not to be distracted by the sun shining through the windows. The stacks of paperwork were the major focus of his morning and the sunshine was not helping his efforts to concentrate. Suddenly his phone rang, jarring him out of the hypnotic state.

"Agent Jones," RJ said.

"Agent Jones, I never thought I'd hear that title."

"Who's calling?" RJ inquired.

"It's your mentor, son."

RJ recognized the voice as soon as the derogatory label of 'son' reached his ears.

"Is this retired Special Agent in Charge, Orville Mann?"

"Very good agent, I knew I had taught you right."

RJ reached down under the edge of his desk and flipped a switch which activated a light on a computer screen in the surveillance room of the FBI building. Subsequently, the agent monitoring the room placed calls to senior agents in other parts of the building and turned the phone recording system on.

"I thought you had dropped off the face of the earth, Agent Mann, what's it been a year since we've spoken."

"Actually, a year and a half, but twenty five years in the bureau, and some personal tragedies, I had to step away from the whole ball of wax and take a long breather," Mann said.

"Personal tragedy?" RJ inquired without trying to sound too nosy.

"My wife lost her three year battle with cancer, shortly after I retired."

"Oh, I'm so sorry to hear that sir."

"That's life; you don't always get the good stuff, so tell me about your life, Agent Jones," The phone clicked.

It took about six months to decide, but eventually I thought the FBI would be a good career choice. But I decided to avoid the rat race of Vegas and stay in Phoenix, close to home.

"How did the academy treat you?" Mann asked.

"It was tough, but it was hardest on my family, to be away for so long."

"It's gotta be done."

"How about you? Still living in Vegas?" RJ asked.

"You know I never really got used to the heat of that place, so I got myself a nice small place outside of Anchorage," Mann responded.

"Your kiddin', Alaska?"

"One and only, can't beat it, plenty of fresh air, open spaces and no hassles."

"That's kinda pricey up there, I've heard."

"You know, I was lucky, my wife and I had good life insurance policies."

"Yeah I really have to do that soon, I've been too busy recently."

"Hey the biggest reason I called is because I been out of touch up here and I was wondering what happened with that casino caper and those two brothers."

"The Scapalini's?" RJ asked, knowing that much of this conversation was rhetorical.

"Yeah."

"You have been out of touch, those two killed themselves. The casino was sold to some big wigs from Vegas and the case was pretty much dropped."

"Nobody else implicated?"

"Nope, both the bad guys died. The girl that got flushed out of that canyon somehow stumbled on the murder, it was the most incredible coincidence."

"What happened to that girl?"

"Her luck changed, considerably. She got medical treatment for her depression. Her husband is still with her and helping her through that. Then she tracked down her deceased father's family who were quite wealthy, but they wouldn't speak to her, because so many other's had come looking for money. So she got legal counsel, did the DNA work and ended up with a pretty little settlement. Her and Jason traveled to Spain and France so she could visit her roots and he could do some world class rock climbing. I still get a card from them once in a while.

The phone clicked again.

"Well I'm running low on quarters here RJ, I'm going to have to say goodbye, but I"ll try and stay in touch in the future."

"Yes sir," RJ said stunned that Mann had used his name at all, "you take it easy up there in the frozen north," then he chuckled slightly and said, "don't let any of those grizzlies get you.

"I'd rather deal with them, than rattlesnakes, take it easy RJ."
The phone clicked for a final time and RJ set the receiver down. Thirty seconds later two senior FBI agents, walked into RJ's office.

"What do ya think?" the first one asked.

RJ leaned back in his chair with his fingers interlaced behind his head, "Well I didn't get a trace on it, but it certainly sounded like him."

"Any background noises you could pick up?" the other agent asked.

"Just some muffled stuff, I'll listen to the tape and see if anything jumps out. It was a pretty lousy connection so I think it may be a pay phone, maybe international.

"What's our next step?" the second agent asked.

"You know we really can't put too many resources into this," the first senior agent responded, "There's really no one screaming for justice; just a possible rogue agent, but we have no definitive proof of that."

Suddenly, an agent burst through the door and blurted out, "We need you right now, sir. Some kind of explosion just occurred in one of our buildings in Oklahoma, it's all over the air waves."

The high humidity and smell of urine even made Orville Mann a little queasy; he couldn't believe the stupidity of people to urinate in a phone booth. A couple times during the call he wanted to open the door of the phone booth, but the ocean was too close and the sound of the waves could have easily been picked up by the sensitive recording equipment on the other end. Finally he got the information he needed, hung up and threw the door open to a fresh breeze of warm salty air. He quickly walked across the sandy beach and out on the rickety dock to a small rubber dingy tied up there.

Stepping into the dingy he said, "Franklin lets go home, son."

The young black man with dreadlocks said," Yes sir, captain."
Then he fired up the outboard motor and the pair motored out to a medium sized ocean going yacht.

"The world breaks everyone and afterward many are strong at the broken places."
Ernest Hemingway

The End